by Teddi Robinson

To Judy

Teddi Robinson
Jan 17, 2013

a BlackWyrm book
Louisville, Kentucky

DEADLY POSE

A BlackWyrm Book
BlackWyrm Publishing
10307 Chimney Ridge Ct, Louisville, KY 40299

Printed in the United States of America.

ISBN: 978-1-61318-131-7
LCCN: 2012945874

Edited by Julia Gabis
Cover Design by Dave Mattingly

First edition: September 2012

Introduction

I had to do some research on the rescue of Mack when he jumped from the plane, and the ripcord to the parachute broke. I had seen the Blue Angels jump from planes, manage to open their chutes, and hold each other's hands in a circle. I felt this could be applied to a daring rescue. My cousin, Bob Campbell, was a paratrooper during the Korean conflict. He was more than happy to help me with this version, including his eye witness account of an attempted rescue once. The two men involved didn't come out as well as Mack and Mr. O'Brien did. One of the gentlemen lost both his legs, and the other man lost his life. Bob said the rescue could be done. I feel that God had a hand in helping with the rescue.

Chapter 1

Joanne looks at Tom and wonders, *Will our plan for the future work? It doesn't seem possible. After all, I'm 14, Tom's 16 and Mary's 12.*

For as long as I can remember, we've met here under this tree. It is so peaceful. I love the creek and the ripples the fish make on the water when they try to grab the insects from the surface.

Mary brought the crackers, Tom the peanut butter, and I brought nothing, but that's the way it is. None of our families has very much, but we share what we have with each other. Believe me when I say sometimes we go hungry, and sometimes we freeze in the winter when we run out of coal. That doesn't matter as the fireplace doesn't heat very well.

"You know what, girls?" Tom asks. "We'll all be millionaires when we grow up, either by hook or crook. Won't we?"

"Yes," we say in unison.

Chapter 2

Ten years later Mary gets off the bus. Joanne rushes to her, gives her a big hug, and asks, "Did you have a good trip?"

"Yes, I did. Have you seen Tom?"

"Now, Mary, you know I have. Tom is the main photographer for The Sunshine Advertising Agency, and I'm the top model for The Straight-laced Model Agency. I see him at least once a week and sometimes more. The agencies work together on a lot of projects. Let's get your luggage and go to the apartment. Then I'll show you the town."

Mary looks at Joanne and says, "I can't wait."

As they walk into the apartment, the phone is ringing. Joanne rushes to the phone, picks it up, answers, and walks into her bedroom.

Mary is dumbfounded but decides to sit on the couch. She thinks, *Wonder what that was about? Is the relationship serious?*

Joanne returns and says, "Sorry, but it was both professional and personal. Tom called to tell me about a photo shoot for tomorrow and to invite us both to dinner tonight."

Twisting her hands, Mary asks, "Are you and Tom involved? If you are, I'll stay at a hotel."

Putting her hands on her hips, Joanne declares, "Don't be ridiculous! I've already told him I'd be at the photo shoot. Now let's get you settled."

"Your apartment is so pretty. Did it come furnished?"

"No, and for two years I've bought pieces as I needed them. Of course my bedroom suite and yours were the first pieces I bought."

"What," Mary says with a laugh, "no refrigerator or stove?"

"They were furnished. Here is your bedroom," Joanne says with a bow and a sweep of her arm. "We share the bathroom. It's between the bedrooms. Hope you don't mind."

"I don't mind at all. It's so nice to be here. Thanks, Joanne, for putting me up."

Putting her arm around Mary, she says, "It's my pleasure. It'll be like old times, sharing the apartment and our lives again. Tom will be here at 8:00, and it's only 5:00 now. If you hurry we can walk and see some of the town."

"I'd like that. The bus ride was very tedious. I sure hope I find a job within a couple of days."

"I'm sure you will," Joanne says as she walks from the room.

***

Joanne looks up as Mary comes out of the bedroom and says, "Mary, you look terrific. That blue dress brings out the color of your eyes, and it complements your red hair. Tom'll want to make a model out of you if you're not careful."

"I wouldn't mind working with Tom, but I don't want to be a model."

The doorbell rings, and Joanne goes to answer it.

Tom enters and, after giving Joanne a kiss on the cheek, says, "Joanne, I want you to meet my brother Mike. He's been away for a long time."

"Glad to meet you, Mike. Come in and meet Mary. We've been friends since childhood. She'll be staying with me for awhile."

"Mary, this is Mike, Tom's brother. I didn't know he had a brother, but I'm glad he has. It'll make the evening more special. Won't it?"

"Mike," Mary says while reaching for his hand to shake, "I'm so glad to meet you, but I'd like to know where you've been. I mean, I've known Joanne and Tom for most of my life, and I never heard about you."

Laughing, Mike says, "You never heard of me because I was never around when Tom was little, and then when we could've run around together, I went to prison."

Mary's eyes get as big as saucers as she lowers her eyelids and says in a whisper, "What did you do?"

"I was the runner and driver for men who made moonshine. I got pulled over for speeding, and I shot the cop. He didn't die, and they didn't connect me with the shooting. A few months later, a revenuer came to the farm looking for a still. Dan, my friend, killed him. I didn't know he could use a gun let alone have one on him.

"I wasn't quite 17 at the time. I didn't realize making and

selling moonshine was illegal or that I would be tried as an adult. The jury found me guilty of association because I was there. They sentenced me to 10 years in prison and 3 years probation. Believe me, I've learned my lesson."

"Oh, my!" Mary exclaims, as she starts wringing her hands. "Are we safe in your company?"

"Yes, you are as safe with me as you would be with your mother."

Joanne says, "Since that's settled, let's go eat. I'm starving."

Tom says, "I made reservations at Hasenour's."

"Good," Joanne says as they leave the apartment.

Chapter 3

"This is a real nice restaurant," Mike says, "and the food is very good. You did yourself proud, little brother."

Tom tells them, "This is one of my favorite places to eat."

Joanne and Mary both nod their heads in agreement. Mary can't hold her curiosity any longer and asks, "Mike, what are you going to do now that you're a free man?"

Hesitating and playing with the food on his plate, Mike answers, "I think I'll find a job here in Louisville and settle down. I'd like to find a nice girl, marry, have children, and become a pillar of the community."

"That sounds like a plan for a lifetime to me. I hope to do the same thing."

Joanne burst out laughing and says, "I'd hope you would want to settle down with a guy and not a girl, Mary."

Blushing, Mary looks at Joanne and says, "You knew what I meant."

"Yes, I did. But you were so serious I just had to insert a little laughter."

Mike takes Mary's hand and says, "I knew what you meant, and I'd like to get to know you a lot better. Where do you want to go to work?"

Removing her hand, Mary says with a twinkle in her eye, "I really don't care as long as I'm in contact with a tall, dark, handsome, rich, single man. You only rate on three of my four requirements."

Becoming very serious, Mike looks at her and says, "If you're patient enough, I'll meet the fourth requirement in a very short time."

"Really?" Mary asks, "What are you going to do, rob a bank? I'd hate to be the lady in red."

"No, I'm not going to play John Dillinger, so you can forget about the red dress."

"Good, but how do you intend to become rich?" Mary asks as she bats her eyelashes.

"The salesmen at various establishments make a lot of money. They work on commission, and usually they sign a contract stating what their salary and commission will be. I've always been able to talk anyone into anything ... even in prison, I could settle disputes without violence."

Mary is thoughtful and then she looks at Mike and says, "Since we are both looking for work, why don't we check with each other every few days to see how we're doing?"

Laughing Mike says, "Gee, I thought you'd never ask."

Tom looks from one to the other, "You two had better eat, or they may start charging us rent on the room."

They all laugh.

Chapter 4

Mary comes bursting through the door and calling, “Joanne! Joanne! I’m home, and I’ve got great news! Where are you?”

Coming from the bedroom, Joanne answers, “I was on the phone. Now what is the great news?”

“I start to work tomorrow at Bank of Louisville. I’ll be in the typing pool for the president, vice president, and the other officers of the bank. Isn’t that wonderful? I guess we did get a good education from the Red Bird Mission, didn’t we?”

“That is wonderful news. Yes, the Red Bird Mission prepared us for life outside of the mountains. They were strict, but it paid off. It seems that everyone who went there and left the mountains has found a very successful life.”

“I hope that is true for me. It seems to be true for you and Tom. I want to make a very good impression tomorrow. Please help me select an outfit to wear on my first day.” Mary then walks to her bedroom, and Joanne follows.

Opening her closet, Mary takes out a black dress trimmed in white. Holding it up to herself, she asks, “Do you think this will be okay?”

“Black isn’t very flattering to you, but I understand the bank is very conservative. They will want you to wear dark clothes or at least a dark skirt with a white blouse and dark jacket. The white collar on that dress with the white cuffs on the sleeves should enhance your fair skin. Your hair will be accented by the dark colors, and it definitely will bring out the blue in your eyes. Not to mention that the dress is a princess style and will accent your figure properly. Yes, by all means wear it. Are you going to wear white or black shoes?”

“I think black shoes. The white would stand out, and I’m sure they wouldn’t appreciate it one bit. Also, I’ll wear a black, pillbox hat, a black purse, and white gloves.”

"And I think you'll be the envy of every girl in the typing pool. Good luck tomorrow. I have a photo shoot tomorrow morning, so we can walk together, if you would like."

"Oh, Joanne, I'm so happy. I feel like dancing. Where could we go?"

Laughing Joanne says, "Without escorts, nowhere. We could call Tom and Mike and have them take us. However, we couldn't stay out very long because we don't want you going to work with bags under your eyes, do we?"

Mary gives Joanne a playful slap on the arm and says, "Killjoy. Okay. I'll be good and stay home."

"Good, then we can celebrate this weekend with the boys."

The phone rings, and Joanne goes to answer it. Mary hears part of the conversation and is startled when Joanne says, "I'll see if she is in. Please hold on a moment."

"Mary, it's someone from the bank. Do you want to talk to him?"

"Get his name and phone number. Tell him I'm in the shower and will have to call him back."

Turning back to the phone, Joanne writes down the name and phone number.

Mary looks at the paper and says, "That's the personnel manager. I wonder what he wants. Surely he isn't going to renege on the job."

"I don't think so. He probably wants to ask a question about your application. One thing's for sure: You won't know until you call him back."

Running her hand through her hair, Mary says, "You're right. Has enough time elapsed for me to get out of the shower?"

Joanne laughs and says, "Yes, dummy, you could have been drying off. Now call him before I do."

Laughing, Mary picks up the phone and dials. After a slight pause, Mary says, "Hello, this is Mary Jones, and I believe you called me.

"Yes, yes, I can. Thank you. I'll be there at 8:00 tomorrow morning.

Thank you again and goodbye."

Mary stands for a few minutes just looking at the phone. Finally, Joanne walks over and gently shakes her.

Joanne says, "Surely you didn't get fired this quickly. Did you?"

"Would you believe, I'm to be the president's private secretary?

His regular secretary was taken to the hospital this afternoon and isn't expected to come back to work for several weeks. Boy, this is happening way too fast. I haven't started work yet, and I've already gotten my first promotion."

Joanne puts her arms around her and says, "They thought you were the most qualified applicant. I'm so proud of you."

***

Mike enters the apartment and sees Tom sitting at the kitchen table with a cup of coffee.

"Hey, Tom. I got a job with On Time Trucking. They do local deliveries, and I start tomorrow. Mr. Wingate told me he could use a man who could drive on any kind of roads, and since I delivered moonshine that makes me qualified.

"I asked if I had to do anything illegal, and he said no. Can you believe it? Maybe I'll learn enough about the trucking business and make enough money to start my own company. Wouldn't that be something?"

Looking straight ahead with a glassy look, Mike adds, "Maybe I'll make enough to ask Mary to marry me!"

Tom shakes his head. "I wouldn't count on that. She made her mind up a long time ago to marry someone rich. It'll take you a long time to accumulate enough money to please her. Better look somewhere else for a wife."

Glancing at the floor, Mike takes a deep breath and says, "I don't want to look anywhere else, and she could change her mind. Maybe she could dream with me and help me with my plans to own my own trucking firm."

Tom just shakes his head and says, "Maybe. Good luck, pal."

Mike looks at his watch and exclaims, "I've got to call Mary. I told her I'd call the minute I got a job. How about I ask her out to celebrate?"

"Oh, go ahead. Do you want to make it a foursome?"

"I'll ask Mary, and if she says yes then you can come."

Chapter 5

Joanne is sitting on the couch when Mary returns from work.

"How was your first day at the bank?" Joanne asks

"Oh, Joanne," Mary says, "you won't believe my day or my discoveries. Providence is really looking out for us."

Laughing, Joanne says, "Okay, give. I know you met the president because they told you Friday that you'd be his secretary. So what else is new?"

"Well, for one thing he's very handsome. He's single but still grieving over the death of his wife of 17 years. He has a son, age 15, who is very intelligent. They enjoy hiking, camping, church, and visiting friends."

"He sounds perfect. Does he have any money? How did his wife die? Does his son live with him, or is he in a private school? I need to know a lot more about him before I want to meet him. Maybe you'd rather date and marry him yourself."

"No, Joanne. I wouldn't," and lowering her eyes she adds, "If someone else had more money, nobody could turn my head."

"Well, well. I bet I can guess who that person is."

"Oh, Joanne, this isn't what I planned, but I think I've fallen in love with Mike. He is so nice and easy to talk to, and I enjoy his company. I wish he had more money, but then if we both worked hard and saved maybe it would work out. We could buy a company or start one of our own. It wouldn't be instant riches but a steady growth and maybe for me -- us -- it would be the best."

"What an idealist. It sure sounds good." Joanne rises from the couch and starts for the kitchen. "I wish you luck."

Mary follows Joanne to the kitchen and says, "You haven't told me about your day. So give."

"It was just the usual. I posed for pictures for a new ad, and Tom took the photos. These were taken at Cherokee Park. I love the scenery and the serenity. I like to go to the top, sit on a bench, and watch the people. There is always somebody walking or riding a bike, and it's always quiet."

"Joanne, it sounds wonderful. Could you show it to me after supper?"

"It's a little far to walk, but maybe tomorrow we could get sandwiches and go. We could invite the boys and have a mini picnic. We could walk to Central Park today."

"Okay. Let me put on my walking shoes, and I'll be ready."

Just then the phone rings, and Joanne answers.

"Mary, it's for you." She hands the phone to Mary and walks into the other room.

"Mike," Mary says, "that's great news. I'd love to celebrate with you, but Joanne and I were about to walk to Central Park and then stop for a sandwich on the way home.

"I'm sure Joanne wouldn't mind, but hold a minute and I'll ask her."

Mary walks to the bedroom door and says, "Joanne, Mike got a job and wants to celebrate. Would you mind if he and Tom joined us on our walk?"

"Of course not. Tell them to pick us up in an hour."

"Okay."

***

"This is great," Mary tells them. "I'm so glad you thought to pick up sandwiches and drinks before you came over. I love picnics even if we do have to drive."

Mike shakes his head and says, "I can't take the credit. It was all Tom's idea."

Tom laughs and says, "I knew the food in the park would be a hit. This is the closest we've come to the woods back home. We used to bring food to the hill that over looked the creek; we'd sit there eating and dreaming of our futures. It looks like we're on our way to realizing our dreams. Doesn't it?"

Joanne takes Tom's hand and tells him, "Yes, and Mary is going to introduce me to her boss in a few weeks. He is the president of the Bank of Louisville. Isn't that great?"

Tom wrinkles his brow, looks deep into Joanne's eyes, and says, "I'm not sure I like the idea. I kinda like it just the way it is ... just the two of us." After some thought, he adds, "Of course you may not want it to be just the two of us."

Joanne tells him, “Tom, I love you as a friend, and I always will, but I don’t want to struggle like I did as a child for everything I want. I want nice things and lots of money.”

“Very well, Joanne. We’ll see what the future brings.”

Chapter 6

"Joanne," Mary says as she enters the kitchen, "Please pour me a cup of coffee, and I'll tell you my exciting news of the day."

Laughing, Joanne reaches for the coffee pot and says, "Don't tell me that Mike proposed, and you accepted."

"No, and I wouldn't accept anyway. He doesn't have enough money ... yet. Anyway, my exciting news is ... the bank is going to have a large advertising campaign. I'm not sure who will get the account, but I'm going to suggest The Sunshine Agency. And you know who will be the model, don't you?"

"That would be nice, and I could meet your boss without your involvement. Of course, the bank may not go with Sunshine, and if they do they may have their own employees do the talking and modeling."

"I have a lot of influence, and that's not going to happen."

Scratching her head, Joanne says, "I could tell Tom of the plans, and he could tell his boss. Then the wheels would be set in motion and Sunshine would be the first agency to contact the bank."

Rising to her feet and walking to the phone, Mary turns and says, "I'll call Mike and ask him and Tom to supper tonight. I know it's short notice, but I think it's urgent. Don't you?"

"Yes, and I'm sure the guys will agree."

***

Sitting on the couch with her legs under her, Joanne says, "We invited you over tonight because we have some important news."

Tom looks deep into her eyes and asks, "Did you decide that you didn't want to be millionaires and Mary is going to marry Mike?"

"Let's get serious," Mary exclaims.

"No." Joanne says. "We have some great news that will benefit us all. The bank is going to launch a huge advertising campaign, and we want you to let your boss know so you will get the job."

Rising, Tom starts pacing the floor. "I don't have to because Sunshine has a contract with the Bank of Louisville to do all its advertising."

Rushing to him, Joanne throws her arms around him and exclaims, "That's great! When do we start shooting?"

Laughing, Tom gives her a hug and says, "Hold on a minute. The bank will notify us, and we'll start on the advertising immediately. After several meetings, the bank will decide on the campaign and then Sunshine will tell me when, where, and what time to be at the location. They will also tell me what the idea is, so I can decide what model to use and how I want to take the pictures."

Joanne puts her hand up to her chin and thoughtfully says, "I didn't realize that you had so much responsibility. I thought all you had to do was take pictures."

Tom says, "Most people don't realize how demanding a photographer's responsibilities are. If we make a mistake, it damages our career. If you make a mistake, you can correct it. I can't. The picture stays around forever to remind everyone that I did a horrible job."

Joanne kisses him on the cheek and lowering her voice says, "I won't try to tell you your job again, and I'll do as you say."

Tom holds Joanne and tells her, "That's the best news I've heard all day."

Joanne pulls away and gives him a playful slap on the cheek.

Tom in mock anger rubs his cheek and says, "The last girl that did that is now retired, married, and has a couple of kids. Would you like to do the same?"

They all laugh and change the subject.

Chapter 7

Joanne is sitting by the amphitheatre in Iroquois Park when Tom walks over with a very handsome man.

Tom says, “Joanne, I want you to meet Mr. Mack Stevens. He’s the president of the Bank of Louisville, and he will describe what he is trying to convey.”

Extending her hand, Joanne looks into Mack’s eyes and says, “It’s nice to meet you. I’m Joanne. Please tell me what you want me to do.”

“As you know, Joanne, we are trying to attract new customers with this ad. You will be the focal point and the voice of the bank. I appreciate the fact that you wore a conservative outfit. You have the look of a bank officer.”

“Thank you, Mr. Stevens. I promise to do my best. Please do not hesitate to make suggestions.”

Walking away, Mack is thinking, *I wonder if it’s too soon after Julie’s death to think of dating again. I think I’d like to get to know Joanne better. She would be an asset on any man’s arm ... so why not mine? After the pictures are taken, I’m going to ask her out for coffee.*

Mack is watching and admiring Joanne from a lawn chair. He hasn’t made any suggestions and is mesmerized by her beauty and graceful movements.

Tom takes another picture and tells Joanne, “Please, stand at the side, tilt your head, put one hand on your hip, and the other hand on your chin. Now look questioningly at the stage like you can’t quite figure out what it is or who you want to perform on it.”

“Tom, I’m not a contortionist. Let me show you what I think the pose should be.”

“And you said, and I quote, ‘I promise not to tell you what to do.’”

Laughing, Joanne says, “You’re right, but I do think this will be better. Why don't we let Mr. Stevens decide?"

"Good idea." Tom turns to Mack and says, "Mr. Stevens, we have a disagreement on this next shot. We'd appreciate it if you would give us your opinion."

"I'd like that," Mack says as he gets up from the chair and walks over to Tom.

Joanne stands the way Tom told her to and then she stands her way. She turns her back to the camera and puts one hand on her chin while tilting her head to the side.

Mack looks at Joanne and says, "Would you mind a third suggestion?"

Together, they both say, "No."

Mack sits down about middle of the first row of seats and says, "Why don't you sit about here and then let's have that quizzical look from you."

"That's a great shot. Thanks, Mr. Stevens. I'll have these developed in no time flat." Tom shakes Mack's hand and turns to Joanne. "Thanks for a great shoot. I'll see you at 2:00."

"Looking forward to the next time," and Joanne starts to walk away.

"Joanne," Mack calls, "I'd like a word with you, before you leave."

"Of course," and Joanne turns and walks toward Mack.

"Yes sir?" she asks, "How may I help you?"

Tilting his head to one side, Mack looks like a kid who just got caught with his hand in a cookie jar. He looks at Joanne and says, "You'll have to forgive me, but it has been a long time since I've asked for a date. You are so beautiful that I feel like I'm 16. Anyway, I would like to buy you a cup of coffee."

Knowing she can't antagonize the customer, she tells him, "I'd love to have a cup of coffee, but I can't stay long as I have another shoot at 2:00."

"That's fine, I promise I'll have you back in time." Mack offers his arm to Joanne, and they go to his car.

***

Mary rushes into the apartment, and calls "Joanne, where are you?"

Joanne comes from the kitchen and asks, "What's all the excitement? Is the building on fire? What?"

"I need to hear about your spur-of-the-moment coffee date. What did you talk about? Did he ask you for a real date? Come on, give."

Joanne laughs and says, "My, but you're full of questions, aren't you? Yes, he did ask me to join him for supper this evening. As for our conversation, that's private. He did tell me about his son and how his wife died. I felt sorry for him. Did you know that she was his private secretary, and that's how they met?"

"No, I didn't. Maybe I should have made him fall for me instead of you."

Joanne laughs and tosses her head. "I don't think you're his type. Anyway, I think I have a good chance of marrying him. If I do, then I'll be your boss' wife, and I can boss you around."

Mary gives Joanne a playful shove and says, "You are the first person he has asked out since his wife died, so watch it. He may become the man around town and date every single girl in the bank including me."

"Don't you worry," Joanne says with a twinkle in her eye. "I'll see that doesn't happen. Anyway, I've spent too much time talking with you. Mack is picking me up at 7:00."

Chapter 8

Tom, Mike, Mary, and Joanne are sitting around the kitchen table in Joanne's apartment. Joanne says, "I can't believe I've been dating Mack for a year. Can you?"

Tom answers, "I can. It kills me every time you have a date with him. Joanne, let's forget being millionaires and just go back to being ourselves. Mary and Mike could get married and save towards starting their own business. What'd ya say?"

Joanne slams her fist on the table and screams, "NO, ABSOLUTELY NOT! I will not live like I did during my childhood. I will marry Mack, and then we'll see what happens."

Mary turning towards Joanne says, "There's no reason to get so upset. I know for a fact that Mack thinks a lot of you. It wouldn't surprise me to see an engagement ring within the next few weeks."

Mike tells them, "If I could have broken this vow of becoming millionaires, I would have a long time ago. I'd marry Mary in a minute, but she wants money more than she wants me. By the way. Mary, I now have $3,000 in the bank. I know that isn't enough for you, but I will have a lot more, sooner than you, or anyone else, thinks."

Having calmed down a little, Joanne tells them, "Well, even if Mack and I do marry, I'll still keep my job, and that means posing for Tom anytime he calls."

Grinning from ear to ear, Tom says, "I'm glad to hear that. I don't want to lose ... working with you."

Mike looks from one to the other, and with a puzzled look on his face asks, "Are you two involved more than you're willing to admit?"

In unison they both answer, "No."

"Well," Mike says, "it seems like you are."

Mary rises from the table and says, "Does anyone need another cup of coffee?"

Laughing, Joanne tells them, "That's a good way to change the subject, isn't it?"

Mike looks adoringly at Mary and says, "I think we all need a refill. Is there any cake left? I'd like a piece if there is."

"Yes," Joanne says and she rises from the table.

With the cake and coffee served, Mike tells them, "I was going to tell you all next week, but I've decided to tell you now. I'm up for this year's safety award. If I win, it'll mean a nice bonus for me and a raise in the amount I receive for each mile I drive. You know I work on a base amount, and the award would mean my base would be larger." After a small pause, he continues, "See, Mary, I'll probably have the money you want before you meet your millionaire."

Mary lowers her eyes, puts her hands in her lap and says, "I keep hoping." Then with a laugh she adds, "Maybe my rich uncle will die in the poor house and leave his millions to me."

They all laugh.

Chapter 9

Joanne is taking off her shoes when the phone rings. Answering, she is surprised to hear Mack's voice.

"Hello.

"I think that would be nice.

"Yes, I'll be ready at eight.

"I'll see you then," and she hangs up the phone.

Mary enters the door and, seeing a puzzled look on Joanne's face, asks, "What's the matter? Did you get a terrible phone call? What happened?"

Joanne answers, while twisting her hair, "No to all your questions. Mack asked me to supper and requested that I wear something extremely nice. He didn't say where we were going and acted very strange. He probably has a business meeting and wants someone on his arm to charm the other man's wife."

Rushing to Joanne's side, Mary takes her hand and says, "I don't think so. At least I don't know of a meeting tonight with anyone, and I always know of his business engagements."

"Guess, I'll have to wait and see. Won't I?"

"Yes, you will, but I bet he is going to pop the question. What will you tell him if he does?"

Joanne gets up and walks to the window. She twists her hair again and says, "I'll ask for a few days to think it over. I don't want to act over anxious."

Mary shakes her head and tells her, "I wouldn't wait too long to say yes. He may get impatient and look for someone else."

"You could be right," Joanne says as she walks to the kitchen.

***

"Mack," Joanne says, "The evening has been perfect. Thanks for asking me out. I had a great time."

"Well, my love," he says, "it isn't over yet. Let's walk for a while. I need to talk to you unless you need to get home."

"No, Mack, I'm not in a hurry for the evening to end."

"Good," Mack says as he reaches for her hand.

They walk for several blocks without saying a word, each lost in their own thoughts. Joanne thinks, *I wonder when he's going to tell me what is on his mind. Could he be working up the courage to ask me to marry him? I hope so. Wonder if I'll have the nerve to make him wait several days for my answer.*

Mack is thinking, *She is so beautiful and talented. I wonder if she would be willing to give up her modeling career to become my wife. I guess I'll never know unless I ask her.* He takes a deep breath and clears his throat. "Joanne, I think I fell in love with you the moment I saw you. I know how much you enjoy your career, but I'm hoping that what I'm about to tell you will convince you to give it up." He stops, looks at the ground, and feels like a teenager. He takes her in his arms and gives her a kiss. "Joanne, I'm at a loss for words, but I'd like for you to consider marrying me. Will you?"

Joanne gives him a quick kiss on the cheek and says, "The thought is very tempting, but I need time to think about it. I really like my life the way it is, and I'm not sure I could live up to your expectations."

"Honey, if you did nothing except sit in a chair and wait for me to come home, that would be enough. However, I would want you to quit work because as my wife there would be certain requirements. You'd have to become part of the banking community and be an example to all the other ladies in town. You'd have to joing and take an active part in certain clubs and organizations. There would be volunteer work, and we'd have to give parties for friends, business associates, and employees. I'd expect to plan these events, but you'd also oversee the help, whether it's caterers or waiters. Of course you are expected to be at my beck and call at all times. I know this is a lot to ask, but I don't want to live without you by my side."

"It's a lot to think about," Joanne says. "I'll have to make a list of advantages and disadvantages. Could I give you my answer tomorrow?"

"Of course, Darling, and I'll be on pins and needles until then."

They walk the rest of the way in silence.

***

Mary is asleep, but Joanne needs to talk, so Joanne shakes her awake.

Mary rubs the sleep from her eyes, stretches, and asks,."What's the matter?"

"You were right!" Joanne exclaims. "He asked me to marry him. Now what do I do?"

"Remember the plan? If you do, then the answer must be yes. However, if you and Tom are involved, and you don't want to give him up, then the answer must be no. Which is it going to be?"

Joanne lowers her eyes and says, "I think I'll talk it over with Tom, before I give Mack my answer."

"I wouldn't wait too long. May I go back to sleep?"

Absently, Joanne answers, "Sure," and goes to her room.

Chapter 10

Tom knew that Mack was going to propose. He's anxious to talk to Joanne, but doesn't want to call her at home. He thinks, *I'll see her this afternoon. Then I'll know if he proposed or not. I wish I had the money. She wouldn't get a chance to marry anyone but me. Oh well, maybe he won't live long and then we'll be together ... I hope.*

The phone rings, and Tom rushes to answer. "Hello.

"Yes, this is he.

"I'm sorry Mack, but I won't see her 'til this afternoon.

"I'll do what I can. I really can't promise anything except I'll try.

"Okay, I'll call you as soon as the shoot is over.

"Sure, I know how you feel. 'Bye for now."

Scratching his head and hanging up, Tom stands and stares at the phone. *I wonder if she is waiting to talk to me. What will my advice be? I'll get ready for this afternoon. Maybe I should pray about it. Think I'll get a cup of coffee first.* He then walks to the kitchen.

Before he reaches the kitchen, the phone rings again. Tom turns and walks back to the phone.

"Hello?

"Well, I didn't expect to hear from you until this afternoon.

"Yes, we'll go for coffee after the shoot. By the way Mack called me awhile ago. I'll tell you about it over coffee.

"'Bye, Joanne, until later."

Boy! Tom thinks, *Am I the great confessor or what? Mack wants me to talk Joanne into marrying him, and she wants my advice on whether to marry him or not. I sure wish we hadn't made the pact to be millionaires when we were kids. This afternoon should be interesting, to say the least.*

***

Sipping her coffee, Joanne says, "Mack asked me to marry him last night. I'm not sure I want to. He does have a 16-year-old son, and I'm not sure if I'm qualified to raise someone else's child. What do you do to entertain a 16- year-old boy? Could I even be a good mother ... or wife for that matter? Oh, Tom, what am I to do?"

Taking her hand in his, Tom looks into her eyes and says, "Hey, we wanted to become millionaires, and you have the first chance to become one. I didn't count on falling in love with you, but this is a golden opportunity. You did say he likes to camp and hike, didn't you?"

"Yes, he does. He wants me to quit working, and I'm not sure I would fit in with the gardening crowd or with the country club set. I've never worked on a project to raise money or planned a dinner party for more than three people, plus myself. What if I gave my career up and wasn't a success at being a wife and mother? If he left me, would I be able to pick my career up again? Help me, please, Tom."

"You're a quick learner, and I'm sure you'd be a success at anything you put your mind to. Marry the guy, but tell him you must keep your hand in the working world. I'm sure he'll let you take a few assignments from time to time. Of course you'll have to meet all his requirements first. Do you think it'd be worth a try?"

"But what about us? Would you be willing to wait for me 20 or 30 years?"

"Honey, I'd wait a lifetime for you, if I had to. Since he likes to hike, and Mary will be your maid of honor, we could go on a camping trip to Natural Bridge State Park. There are a couple of very steep crevices on the trail. He might have an accident. Then we'd be set for life. Set your goal to become his wife and beneficiary on a very large insurance policy. Make friends with his son, have Mary and me come to supper often, get him to invite us on a camping trip, and then leave everything to me."

"So you really think I should plan my wedding?"

"Yes, I do., The quicker, the better."

Rising from the table, Joanne kisses him on the cheek and says, "I've got to run. Mack is picking me up at 7:00. We're going to eat, and then we'll take a walk while I give him my answer."

"Okay. I'll see you at the next shoot."

Chapter 11

Joanne puts on a blue satin dress with white heels. She fixes her hair and applies her makeup with extreme care. She is ready to leave when Mack comes to pick her up at 7:00.

Mack takes one look and whistles softly. He takes her in his arms and gives her a kiss. Holding her away from him, he looks at her in appreciation and says, "You are beautiful. I'm so lucky to have met you. Have you thought about my proposal? I don't want to rush you, but I'm anxious to know the answer."

"I've put a lot of thought into this and I'd love to be your wife and a mother to your son ... but I have a condition before I say yes. I do need to keep my hand in modeling. I hope you understand. I really don't want anyone to say I married you for your money. I know I'm not, and I hope you know it also. Anyway, I wouldn't work as much as I do now, and I'll try to be the perfect wife," she continues with a laugh, "if that's possible."

Mack takes her in his arms, gives her a long, sweet kiss and says, "You've made me the happiest man alive, and yes you can work part time. As long as you are at my side when I have to entertain and you have time for the required social meetings. Let's eat, and then let's look at rings and plan our engagement party. We need to set a date. I'll have to look at the bank's calendar. We don't want our wedding and honeymoon to conflict with any of the bank's functions. Do we?"

"I guess I'll have to get used to the fact that the bank comes first in everything, won't I?"

Grinning from ear to ear, Mack says, "Yes, my dear, I'm afraid so." He takes Joanne in his arms and gives her another kiss. The kiss tells Joanne that he will always take care of her.

"I'm so excited, I'm not sure I can eat a thing! Honey, do you mind if we cancel our reservation and look at rings first?"

"Of course not," Joanne replies,

Mack goes to the phone and calls over his shoulder, "I'll call Ben Benedict. He should still be at the store. I know he'll wait for us, and then we'll eat."

"Okay."

***

Looking at her ring, Joanne says, "Thanks so much, but I wouldn't have spent that much on something that everyone will look at and either criticize or envy."

"I want them to be envious of the beautiful, gracious, loving angel I'm going to marry. Joanne, I'm so in love with you that anything, *anything,* you want, I'll try my best to get for you."

Joanne asks, "How did I get so lucky as to have you fall in love with me?"

"By being you," Mack answers.

"Oh, Mack, do you think your son will accept me?"

"He already has. He keeps asking, 'When are we going to keep her?'

"I told him I was going to ask you to marry me, and he has bitten his fingernails down to the quick waiting for your answer. I guess I should call him, but he'd want me to bring you home so he could gush all over you. I don't want to share you with him tonight."

Laughing, Joanne reaches for his hand and says, "I hope I'm not going to have to referee the two of you for the rest of my life."

"I'll see that you don't. Now, back to business. When do we have the engagement party?"

"I think next month would be nice, don't you?"

Mack scratches his head and asks, "Do you think you can plan a party for 500 people in that short amount of time?"

"Of course," Joanne says, laughing, "unless you are going to invite the Queen of England or the President of the United States."

Matching her laughter, Mack tells her, "I would invite both of them along with their spouses, if I thought they'd come." After a moment's silence, he says, "Let's stop by the bank, and I'll look at the calendar. Then we can set a date for the party. Okay?"

"Yes. That'd be great."

***

Walking into Mary's bedroom Joanne looks at the sleeping girl.

She leans down and gently shakes her while saying softly, “Mary, please, Mary, will you wake up?”

Rolling over and rubbing the sleep from her eyes, Mary says, “No, I don’t want to wake up, and you can’t make me.” She then rolls over with her back to Joanne.

“That’s okay,” Joanne says as she starts out of the room. “I thought you might want to be the first to see my ring.”

Mary sits up and calls, “You come back here this instant! How could you think I would rather sleep than see your ring?”

Joanne walks back to the bed and extends her hand.

Mary doesn’t say a thing but takes Joanne’s hand, turns it first one way and then another, letting the light catch the brilliance and the sparkle of the large diamond on her finger. With a twinkle in her eye, she says, “This diamond is so small you can hardly see it. Didn’t they have a larger one?”

Joanne sighs and says, “Make fun if you want to, but remember: When I become a rich widow, I’ll have control of the money. Keep it up, and I’ll see that you work the rest of your life.”

“You wouldn’t dare.” With a laugh, Mary continues, “Are you going to show the ring to Tom? I bet he’ll be impressed.”

“Yes, I am.” Joanne answers.

Chapter 12

Sitting on the couch with her legs crossed under her, Joanne tells Mary, "I still can't believe all the people I have to invite to our engagement party. The list includes all the politicians, their spouses, and anyone who is someone in Louisville. Mack wasn't kidding when he said the engagement party would be for 500 people."

Looking at Joanne and taking a sip of her coffee, Mary says, "This is what you wanted. You knew when you started dating Mack that you'd be thrown in with the society crowd of Louisville, didn't you?"

"Yes, but I wasn't prepared for it to happen so soon. I honestly thought we would have a quiet, small party with just family and a few intimate friends. Boy, was I wrong! I think Mack would rent the largest billboard to announce our engagement if I he could." The phone rings, and Joanne reaches for it.

"Hello?

"Hi, Honey.

"Sure, Mack, should I wear something special? What time should I be there?

"Okay, Dear, I'll see you at 12:00."

Joanne hangs up the phone and stands staring at it.

Mary laughs and says, "I don't think the phone is going to tell you what's on his mind. You'll just have to meet him and be surprised."

Joanne moves away from the phone and says, "I guess you're right. I've got to get ready. He wants me to wear his favorite dress. I'll talk to you later." She starts toward her room.

Mary heads to the kitchen with her cup and calls over her shoulder, "Be sure you do. I want to know every little detail."

Laughing, Joanne heads to the bathroom and says, "You sure are nosy."

***

“The luncheon date was very impressive. Mary, I walked into the bank and saw this group of people over by the elevator. I thought nothing of it and took the stairs. Image my surprise when I reached the top and this group of people started clapping as I came out of the doorway. They were from the various businesses in downtown Louisville. Tom was the first to walk over to me. He said, ‘*The Louisville Times* has decided to do a feature story on your and Mack’s engagement and, of course, marriage. We hope you don’t mind, but each of the men and women here represents either a business or the paper.’ Mary, I was flabbergasted. I think I thanked them, but I’m not sure. Because of the publicity, we’ll get a big discount on anything and everything we buy for the wedding. Isn’t that wonderful?”

Wagging her finger at Joanne, , Mary replies, “Just remember, I want the same deal for my wedding. I think it’s wonderful. Are you going to send the clippings back home?”

“You bet I am!” Joanne exclaims, “They didn’t think I’d amount to anything, and I want them to eat crow.”

“Where did you get your ring?”

. “Buschemeyer’s on Fourth Street,” Joanne says. “It’s the only place in town where everybody who is anybody goes for jewelry.”

“It sure is impressive.”

“We went back to Buschemeyer’swith Tom, and Mr. Benedict showed us rings again. Tom took pictures, including a photo of my hand with the engagement ring on it. I can’t believe this is happening to me. I wonder why we were picked for the story.”

“Because you’re a top model, and Mack is the president of the bank.” Mary says, as she walks from the room.

Chapter 13

Joanne gives a sigh of relief and sits down as the last guest leaves the party. “Mary, how was the party?” she asks.

“I thought it went great. The band was very good, and everyone seems to have had a good time. I didn’t think anyone was surprised by Mack’s announcement of your engagement d,id you?”

“No, I didn’t,” Joanne answers. “You don’t think Mack discussed our marriage with these people before he discussed it with me, do you?”

Sitting down and resting her chin in her hand, Mary says, “Well, I think if I had a teenage child and was thinking of bringing in a stepfather, or in your case a stepmother, I’d ask the opinion of a close friend. There are two reasons: One, I’d want to know if there would be a problem that I couldn’t handle. Two, I’d want to know how to introduce the person into my child’s life without his or her resentment.”

“I guess I’m being selfish, but I didn’t want anyone to know until tonight,” Joanne says. “I just didn’t think of it in those terms. You’re right. If the situation were reversed, I’d ask my friends about my intentions.”

“I think you did when you started to date Mack,” Mary tells her. “Remember, you asked Tom and me if you should set your sights on marriage to him. We told you to go ahead. Just make sure after the wedding to have a $1,000,000 insurance policy taken out with you as beneficiary. We also told you to make sure it would pay if Mack died by an accident.”

Joanne looks startled and says, “Boy, when you put it that way, it sounds so heartless, like I’m a gold digger or something.”

Laughing Mary says, “Now’s a fine time to develop a conscious.”

Joining her in laughter, she says, “You’re right. I do respect Mack a lot, and I think I love him a little.”

"Just wait a minute. That's not part of the plan," Mary says, with eyes blazing. "I don't want to wait 25 or 50 years for my share of the money, and don't you forget it."

"I won't," Joanne replies, "but you and Tom will have to plan everything without me."

"That's fine with us. Just remember, you agreed to this a long time ago." Mary rises from her chair. "I think it's time I found Tom and went home. See you later."

"Okay," Joanne replies, "everything will be taken care of here, so I think I'll find Mack and leave also."

***

Walking Joanne to the door of her apartment, Mack says, "Honey, the party was a huge success. Everyone was complimenting me on my choice of a wife and how gracious you are. I'm so glad you agreed to marry me. Some of the men told me not to wait too long to set our wedding date as you might decide to run off with someone else. I don't think you'd do that ... would you?"

"Why, Mack," she says as she turns and puts both arms around his waist, "how could you even listen to those old, jealous men? I swear, you men gossip worse than the old hens I knew back home. Besides, they were probably teasing you. I love you, and I can't wait for our wedding."

"That's what I wanted to hear. May I come in for a cup of coffee?"

"Of course, Darling," she says. "I hope you remembered to bring the bank's schedule so we can start planning our wedding and our lives."

Mack scratches his head and says, "I think I have it in my inside pocket." Reaching into his jacket, he pulls out a little black book.

Before he can say anything, Joanne takes the book from him and says, laughing, "You won't need this anymore. You, Mister, belong to me!"

Blushing, Mack reaches for the book and stammers, "That is my appointment book, and you, Missy, will not find one woman's name or phone number in it. And you have the nerve to call my friends jealous." Then he laughs.

Joanne flips through the book and then hands it back to Mack.

"You know, Honey," Mack says while reaching for the book, "you did such a fantastic job on the party on such short notice that I think we could get married within six months. What do you think?"

Nodding her head, she says, "Yes, the sooner the better. Oh, Mack, I love you so much, and I'll do everything in my power to make you and Jesse happy. By the way, don't you think we should include him in our plans? I mean, shouldn't he help plan the wedding? I know he could be an usher, but I really want him to do and be more than that. What do you think?

Mack says. "Maybe we should ask him before we plan what he'll be doing."

"Of course. You're right, as always."

Mack looks at his little black book and tells her, "Six months from now is March. Do you want to be a March bride?"

"Would you like a cup of coffee?" Joanne asks as she walks to the kitchen.

Mack follows her and says, "Yes, I'd love a cup. Besides, I'd like to get the date, and some other details settled tonight. Then I'll be ready to answer any and all questions tomorrow."

"Okay." She answers, "I think we should get married in February because *The Louisville Times* is featuring us from our engagement through the wedding, and Valentine's Day is in February."

"Can you plan a wedding in five months?"

"I'm so anxious to become your wife, I could probably plan it in one month."

Mack rises and kisses Joanne. "Okay then, we'll be married in February. Now, I'll consult my book to see if we can do that. "I want to marry as close to Valentine's Day as possible. Okay?"

"The 14th comes on Saturday this year," Joanne says excitedly. "What does your little black book say?"

Just as excited, Mack says, "I can delegate everything for that week and the next two weeks to someone else. Not only can we get married on Valentine's Day, but we can take the next two weeks for our honeymoon!"

Joanne asks, "Shall we take Jess out of school and take him with us on the honeymoon?"

Mack looks at her in astonishment. "Whoever heard of taking a child on a honeymoon? I don't think so, but thanks for asking. I haven't decided where we'll go yet. Do you like surprises?"

"Sometimes, if they are nice surprises," Joanne says, and then she looks at Mack with love in her eyes. "I thought maybe we should take Jesse with us. Then he would know that I'm not replacing his mom, and he won't be left out of our lives. Sometimes, a couple does take the children with them. I know one of the guys back home married a lady with four girls, and they took the girls with them so the girls would know they were part of their family."

Mack gazes at Joanne and thoughtfully says, "You're right. Okay, you win. We'll take Jess with us. It looks like we'll be doing family things right from the start."

"Good." Joanne yawns, puts her arms around Mack. "Honey, I'm so tired, and both you and I have to work tomorrow. Could we finish the plans later?"

Mack kisses her and says, "Sure, Honey. You go ahead and get ready for bed. I'll show myself out."

Chapter 14

Looking at herself in the full length mirror, Joanne says, "I can't believe this is happening. Everything for the wedding was paid for by the companies that provided the services. Even my dress and the bridesmaids' dresses were furnished by Greenups. I know I was the model, and the feature stories were about Mack's and my wedding from the day we became engaged, but this is so generous."

Mary answers, "I know. Some people are born with a silver spoon in their mouths, but you just fell into it. That's what you get for being so pretty. How about the honeymoon? Is that paid for also?"

"Yes, it is," Joanne says. "I couldn't believe when *The Louisville Times* announced its intention of running a feature on an engaged couple and their plans to marry, the paper got a notice from Gatlinburg, Tennessee. The town gave us our choice of places to stay as long as the town got, I forgot the amount, in advertising. We have a chalet for three with a kitchen, two bedrooms, and a living room with a fireplace."

Mary straightens Joanne's veil and says, "What will you do there for a week?"

"We plan to hike, shop, and we are to appear at their Toastmaster's breakfast. We'll be featured on one of the radio shows. I've forgotten the call letters and the time. That's Mack's job. The hometown paper has carried our engagement and wedding plans. This is their conclusion. We've become quite the ideal couple -- family -- and the ideal wedding for other couples."

"I think it's fabulous."

After a knock on the door, the bridesmaids come into the room. One of the girls says, "It's time to line up. Everyone's here, and they are getting anxious to see the bride."

The wedding march is being played, and the first girl starts down the aisle.

Everything is perfect, until Joanne starts to put the ring on Mack's finger. She drops it, and it rolls under the first pew. With horror in her eyes, Joanne groans, and Mack laughs. The minister sighs and says, "Never have I seen a bride so nervous."

The ring is recovered, and the wedding proceeds without a hitch.

Joanne, Mack, and Jesse leave for the Smoky Mountains as soon as the reception is over.

***

Jesse stares out the car window, deep in thought. Finally he looks up and says, "Gee, Dad, none of my friends got to go on their father's honeymoon. How come you guys let me come?"

Before Mack can answer, Joanne says, "I wanted you to know that I could never take your mother's place ... nor do I want to. But, I did want to get to know you better and for you to feel that I'm your friend. So, I want us to start being a family right away instead of waiting 'til next week."

"Gee, Joanne, I feel like you are family," Jesse states, as his checks turn a shade of pink.

Mack laughs and tells them, "If Joanne had dropped the ring one more time, I'd have walked away from the marriage before it began."

"That was so embarrassing to me," Joanne states.

Jesse laughs, "If I had seen that on TV, I'd have thought it was funny, but I felt embarrassed for Joanne. The look on her face was funny."

"I know," says Mack, "that's why I laughed. I know one thing, She'll never live that down. I think she was having second thoughts, and it was her way of delaying the ceremony so she could rethink what she was doing."

"Never you mind," Joanne sighs. "I'll catch you both doing something just as stupid. Then the last laugh will be mine ... all mine."

"Dad, we're going to have to watch our step around this evil woman."

"You are so right, son," Mack laughs and looks at Joanne with a wink.

Chapter 15

Joanne walks into the Chalet and thinks, *This is perfect. It's like a picture postcard, surrounded by trees and mountains and with the small creek at the back . True, there isn't a sidewalk, but what the heck! I didn't grow up with sidewalks, and this is so much like home. Someday, I'll have to take Mack and Jesse back to meet my relatives but not anytime soon.*

Mack walks in with his hands and arms loaded with suitcases. He drops them, walks over to Joanne, and takes her in his arms. After kissing her, he says, "You look so pretty, I almost stopped to admire the picture you made. I still can't believe you married me. I think Jesse loves you as much as I do."

Hearing his name, Jesse laughs and asks, "Are you two trying to figure a way to get rid of me already? We just got here. Can I have something to eat first? I'm starving."

"Sure," Mack answers. "We've been planning on getting rid of you ever since we decided to marry. I think we'll start by starving him, don't you, Honey?"

Laughing, Joanne says, "Leave me out of this discussion. Remember, I was in favor of dropping him off at an orphanage. You were the one who wanted to starve him and make his life so miserable that he'd get fed up and leave. Which would you rather we do, Jesse?"

Laughing and scratching his head, Jesse asks, "Can I eat first and then make up my mind?"

In unison they both say, "Yes."

Mack says, "Let's leave the unpacking for later and find a restaurant. They tell me the food here is heavenly. What do you say? Okay?"

Joanne says, "Does this mean I don't have to cook tonight?"

Jesse looks from one to the other and says, "Since I'm on borrowed time here, can I pick the restaurant?"

"Sure, as long as it's not McDonald's," Mack says.

Joanne takes Jesse's hand and tells him, "I second the motion. Now where would you like to eat?"

Jesse says, "I saw a restaurant in the lodge when Dad was checking in. Let's try it. Okay?"

"We'll try anything once," Mack says as he puts an arm around Joanne.

***

"The food was good." Mack says, "In fact, I asked them to put together a picnic basket for three. I'll pick it up at 7:30 tomorrow morning."

Jesse asks, his eyes wide with excitement, "What are you planning for tomorrow? Can I come? Is this when you throw me over a cliff?"

Mack strokes his chin, looks at Joanne and winks. "Son, I'm so glad you asked the last question because we hadn't thought of throwing you over a cliff. That would be ideal. Don't you think so, Joanne?"

"No, I don't," she answers. "What if he didn't die but became crippled? How would we cope? Not to mention he'd have us over a barrel by blackmailing us for everything we have."

"You're right, of course," Mack says. "I guess you'll be safe tomorrow, but watch your step the rest of the time we're here."

"You bet I will," Jesse says, and he sticks out his tongue at them as he leaves the room.

Mack tells Joanne, "We should each pack an extra set of clothes in our backpacks as well as rain gear and a flashlight."

"I didn't realize we might spend the night in the woods." Joanne says.

He looks at her and says, "I hope we don't spend the night, but sometimes accidents do happen, and we need to be prepared. We'll divide the lunch between the three packs, and then no one will have more than they can carry. Okay?"

Crossing the room and sitting down on his lap, Joanne says, "Anything you say is okay with me. I think we are going to enjoy this mini vacation. Do you think Jesse is having fun?"

"Yes, he is. I hope he brought his camera. He has a way with one you wouldn't believe. When we get back home, I'll show you some of his photos."

Joanne kisses Mack and says, “Maybe Tom could use him part time,if he’s good.”

“We’ll see.”

***

Walking into the chalet, the three of them drop their backpacks, and Joanne says, “Okay you guys. We need some heat. Who’s going to start the fire?”

Mack looks at Jesse and walks to the fireplace. “I guess I’ll do it, since Jesse is all wet.”

“Ah, Dad,” Jesse says, “I thought the rocks in the creek would be a short cut. How was I to know it was an optical illusion? The water didn’t look that deep. I bet if I hadn’t gone down to my neck, you guys would’ve followed me.”

Joanne puts her hands on her hips and says, “It’s a good thing we all packed an extra set of clothes. Otherwise, you’d be frozen stiff, and the bears would have a field day.”

“I suggested the extra set of clothes because I did the very same thing the first time I came here,” Mack explains. “There’s nothing like experience to teach you not to make the same mistake twice.”

Jesse starts to laugh and stares at each of them in turn. “Dad, you did tell me to watch my step while I was here. I just didn’t think you’d push me down in the creek to make your point.”

“Did you enjoy seeing the bears?” Mack asks.

“Yes,” Jesse answers, “but I was hoping one of them would chase you or Joanne. That would make a very good picture.”

“Better luck next time.” both Joanne and Mack exclaim.

“If you two are tired of bantering with each other,” Joanne states, “I’d like to know if I should start supper. or will we be eating at the lodge?”

Mack says, “I bought long tongs, and I think you have a can of pork and beans, don’t you?”

“Yes, I do, but what are you proposing, Mack?”

“Well, if we could get Jesse to go to the lodge and buy some marshmallows, then we could have a wiener roast with pork and beans. I think it would be fun, not much work, and we’d still have supper.”

Before Joanne could say anything, Jesse jumps up and says, “I’m on my way.”

"Hold on, Buster," Joanne says. "I think you'll need some money, and we need to decide what we're having for dessert."

"Joanne," Jesse says, "I noticed when we were there last night that they have individual cakes and pies as well as ice cream. Again, no muss or trouble. What kind of cake or pie do you all want?"

Mack walks over to Jesse and hands him $20. "Son, I'm so glad you came with us. I'd have to go to the store if we were alone. Why don't you surprise us, and bring whatever you think we'd like."

"Will do, Dad," and he walks out the door.

Chapter 16

"Well," drawls Tom as he sets up the camera, "how did the honeymoon go?"

Joanne sitting on the park bench says, "Very good. In fact, Tom, I don't know when I've had such a good time. Mack and Jesse interact with each other, and I found myself laughing a lot. Jesse started calling me 'Mom' before we got back home. That is such a lovely feeling. I think I'm falling in love with them both."

Looking very stern, Tom turns toward her and says, "Have you forgotten your agreement with Mary and me, or where we came from? Don't go betraying us now, or you'll live to regret it. How do you think Mack would react if he knew you only married him for his insurance money or that you were in on the plan to murder him? Don't think for one minute I wouldn't tell him."

Joanne looks at Tom with murder in her eyes. "I don't think he'd believe you for one second, but you don't have to worry, I won't renege. It might take longer than you think to pull it off. First, he'll have to agree to the insurance policy. I can't come home from our honeymoon and demand that he take out a $5,000,000 policy, now can I?"

"You're right," Tom says as he turns back to the camera. "I'm impatient."

"After the policy is in place, I think we should go on a camping trip. It can't be to the Smoky Mountains, because that is one of Mack's favorite places. Maybe somewhere else close that has dangerous hiking paths."

Changing the subject, Tom asks, "So what else did you do, besides hike?"

"We played board games, told ghost stories, and ate at the main lodge. They had live entertainment at night, and we even went on a horseback ride and had a camp fire and roasted marshmallows. It was fun, and Jesse has a fine sense of humor. I really enjoyed myself."

Pouting, Tom says, "It sounds like it. After it's all done, you and I will explore the rest of the United States. I'll make your honeymoon memories just that. Believe me, I won't give you up for anyone."

"Remember one thing: I'm married, and I intend to honor my vows. What you and Mary do is your choice. If Mack dies, I will honor my agreement with you two, but just so we're clear, I'll take no part in your plans."

"That's fine with me, as long as I get my share of the money and you. Now let's get to work."

Joanne stands and walks in front of the camera.

Chapter 17

Joanne is setting the table for supper when Mack walks in. He takes one look at the table and frowns. Entering the kitchen, he walks over to Joanne, puts his arms around her waist, and says, “I noticed the table is set for five. Who is coming for supper?”

“Didn’t I tell you?” she asks.

“No, Honey, you didn’t.”

Joanne turns around, gives him a kiss, and says, “I’m sorry, I thought I did. Anyway, Mary and Tom are coming over. Mary is my best friend, and I’d like for you to get to know Tom a lot better. Mary and Tom are a couple, and I think eventually they’ll get married.”

“I doubt it,” Mack tells her. “He’s in love with you.”

“Don’t be ridiculous,” she retorts. “I’ve known both Mary and Tom a long time, and there was never anyone for either of them but each other.”

Mack says, “Honey, I don’t want to call you a liar, but I’ve seen the way he looks at you. He watches every move you make. I still say he’s in love with you, and if something happened to me, he’d drop Mary in an instant.”

“Please, Mack,” Joanne looks into his eyes. “I think you’re jealous. I’m glad because that tells me you love me. Don’t worry. Even if I was free, Tom wouldn’t stand a chance with me. I love you, and I can’t imagine being with anyone else.”

Taking Joanne into his arms, Mack looks into her eyes and says, “I hope you’re telling me the truth, because I want you to quit working all together. You know I never wanted you to work in the first place and only agreed to you working part time. It seems that you are taking more and more assignments and neglecting your social duties more.”

“I’m sorry. I’ll tell Tom not to call me for at least a month. Okay?” Joanne kisses his cheek, slips out of his arms, and walks to the dining room.

Mack follows and says, "We'll see, but I still think he's in love with you."

***

Mary says, "The meal was delicious, Joanne. May I help you clean up?"

"That sounds good, Mary," Joanne answers. "Would you boys like a cup of coffee in the living room?"

"I need to do my homework, so may I be excused?" Jesse asks.

"Sure, Son" Mack answers. "I can't have you skipping your homework, just because we have company, can I?"

"No, Dad, you can't." Turning to the others he says, "I hope you will forgive me, but I have a test in algebra in a couple of days. I'm really having a hard time with it. So, I'll say good night, and it was a pleasure to be with you."

As one, they say, "Good night." Jesse leaves the room.

"Joanne, Tom and I will head to the living room and wait on the coffee. Okay?"

She sticks out her tongue and says, "Your servant will be right in with the coffee, your highness."

Mack laughs at Joanne, turns to Tom, and says, "Let's leave before I get into trouble."

Sitting down in the wing chair beside the fireplace, Mack says, "Tom, I hear that you're busier than ever."

Before Tom can answer, Joanne appears with the coffee and some cookies on a tray. She sets the tray down on the coffee table and leaves without a word.

Tom says, "In answer to your question, yes, I am busier than ever. The pictures I took of your engagement and your wedding put me in high demand. I owe you and Joanne a lot. I don't think I could ever repay you for my success."

"Well, Tom, that's what I need to talk to you about. I know you like to use Joanne as your model, but I feel she is neglecting her duties to me and to Jess. I would appreciate it, if you didn't ask her to model for awhile."

"I'd like to oblige, but the clients always ask for her," Tom says while he strokes his chin, "and I hate to tell them that she isn't available."

"I spoke to Joanne about it before you and Mary came, and she agreed not to take any assignments for at least a month. By that time, I hope you find a model that is as good as Joanne.

"Also, I was wondering when you were going to ask Mary to marry you."

Tom is very uncomfortable and says, "We have discussed marriage. It will take a few more years before we have enough money in the bank to buy a house, and we need enough money to cover us in case of an emergency."

"That sounds reasonable," Mack answers. "By the way, Joanne, Jess, and I are planning a trip to National Bridge State Park in a couple of weeks. We usually stay at the lodge for the weekend and do a lot of hiking. It's always fun. Would you and Mary like to join us? We could get a cabin for five with three or four bedrooms instead of staying at the lodge. What d'ya say? It could be fun."

"If Mary agrees, then I'm all for it. I could take my camera and take some beautiful pictures of the trip." Tom raises his eyebrows in a silent question. "Then I could sell the pictures to one of the magazines with an article."

"I'm not sure if I'm comfortable with you taking pictures of us. We'll discuss that later. Okay?"

"Sure, it was just a thought. I understand Jesse is quite a photographer. I'd like to see his work. Maybe we could work on the photos together."

Frowning, Mack says, "We'll see."

Chapter 18

Turning over in bed to face Joanne, Mack puts his arm around her and draws her close. She opens her eyes, yawns, and snuggles up closer to him. He kisses her and says, "Good morning, Love. How are you this morning?"

"I'm fine, and how are you?" she answers.

Mack kisses her again and says, "It's a beautiful morning. I was wondering if you'd like to go to church. We haven't been since we got married, and I really think we should start going again."

"Jesse has been going. I'm sorry Mack, but I've never been one to go to church. It wasn't something we did in the mountains. We saw God in everything and dedicated everything we did to him. I did go to church when I attended the Red Bird Mission School, but I haven't since."

Rising from the bed, Mack looks at Joanne and tells her, "Well, it's time we start back. This is part of our duty to God, the community, and our marriage. I think we'll start today. Church starts at 11:00 sharp. It's only 9:00 now. We can make it. Afterward, we'll go to lunch and maybe we'll take in a movie this afternoon. Okay?"

Rubbing her eyes, Joanne sits up, looks at Mack, sticks out her tongue and says, "Only if you insist. Go wake Jesse while I take my shower and dress. Do you mind putting the coffee on?"

"Okay, but make it a quick shower and then I'll take mine while you fix breakfast."

Joanne gets out of bed and starts for the bathroom while muttering under her breath, "Why all of a sudden does he want to go to church? He hasn't gone since we started dating, so why now? If I want him to become friends with Tom, I'd better go along with anything he wants, even though it's against my grain. Tom and Mary aren't going to like this turn of events any more than I do. Oh, well, I may even like it, and I can make friends with Mack's friends.

Yes, it could work out to my advantage." She starts humming to herself, and, getting into the shower, she starts singing.

***

Jesse shows the excitement in his face as he says, "This was a great idea, Dad. Some of the girls are in my classes at school. I knew a few of the guys, and they made me feel like I belonged in the Sunday school class. I enjoyed church also. I like what the preacher said about loving one another as you would yourself. The kids invited me to their youth group this evening. They stay for church and then either go to someone's house for cocoa or to a local restaurant. I'd like to go. May I?"

"If it's okay with Joanne, it's okay with me," Mack answers.

"I think that would be great," Joanne says. "It will give you some friends who have morals and will have an influence on the community when they get older. Will someone pick you up or will we need to take you?"

"Thanks, Mom, I'll run back and tell Jimmy that I can go." Turning, Jesse starts to leave and then calls over his shoulder, "I'll be back in a jiffy with your answer."

Watching his son run across the street, Mack turns to Joanne and says, "I haven't seen him this excited about anything since he was five years old. That was the year we bought his bike with the training wheels."

"He's growing up and becoming quite a young man." Joanne states, "You should be extremely proud of him. I know I am. Just think, he'll be 16 next year. He'll want to drive, and have a girl friend and more independence."

"I know," Mack answers, "I'm not sure I want him to grow up."

Laughing, Joanne says, "Time waits for no one, especially the parents of a teenage boy!"

Out of breath coming up to his parents, Jesse says, "They'll pick me up about 6:30. The meeting starts at 7:00, and church lets out at 9:30. They tell me I'll be home before 11:00."

"Good." Mack says, and taking Joanne's hand he starts walking towards the car. "Let's eat and then we'll go home and play some games. Okay?"

"Sounds like fun," Joanne states.

***

"Will you quit pacing the floor?" Joanne asks as she puts her book down. "It's only 10:30. He has another half hour before the time he said he'd be home."

Running his hand through his hair, Mack answers, "I know, but what if something happens to him? It would be my fault because I gave him permission to go."

Joanne gets up and walks over to Mack. She puts her arms around him and says, "Honey, you have growing pains. Jesse is a good boy, and he is with the church group. He'll be on time, and nothing is going to happen to him ... except his growing up to be a fine young man. Now, come on over and sit down. You don't want him to know how anxious you are about him, do you?"

Kissing Joanne on the cheek, Mack says, "No, I don't. When he has kids, then I'll tell him about this night."

Laughing, Joanne leads Mack to the couch. At this moment, the door opens, and Jesse walks in. He walks over to them and says, "Thanks for letting me go with the group. I had a really great time. Jimmy invited me to join his club at school. They are a Christian group and meet every morning for prayer and to discuss the concerns of their lives. Sometimes the discussion is for the improvement of the school. Some of them will be graduating this spring, so they talk about what to do after graduation. I'd like to join them. I think they have a great handle on life, and I know they think God will always bless what they do."

Joanne is the first to speak. "That's a great idea. Your dad and I were talking tonight about you and your next birthday when you hit the big 16. Check with your group to see what the ground rules were when they got their first cars. Ask them how old they were and if they had to buy their own cars and the insurance. I'll check with some of the mothers, and your dad can check with some of his friends. Then we'll compare notes and compromise. Okay? Mack? Jesse?

Mack, grinning from ear to ear, says, "I don't think he should have a car, whether he pays for it or not, until he's 25. Then he'll be out of college and starting his career. Without a car, he'll have to concentrate on his studies and not the girls."

Jesse walks over and gives his dad a playful punch on the arm and says, "That might work if all girls demanded that a guy have a car, but quite a few of the girls in the group look at a guy as a person and not at what he has or hasn't got. I think I can find a girl who would date a guy without a car just because she likes him."

"Well, I could sit and listen to this discussion all night, but we have to get up early in the morning," Joanne says as she rises and stretches. "We'd better get to bed."

Mack walks over and hugs Jesse. "Son, I want you to know how proud I am of you. Yes, you may join the prayer group at school. Joanne made a very good suggestion, and I, for one, intend to follow up on it. We'll compare notes on the car issue in a few days. I love you, but I need my beauty sleep. Good night. Have pleasant dreams."

Chapter 19

"Well, Joanne," Mack says as he sits at the kitchen table, "what have you found out about cars for Jesse?"

Joanne answers, "Not very much. The mothers I've talked to all say the same thing. Their sons worked and saved their money to pay for at least half of the car, and some paid for the total price. All had to pay for their insurance.

"They also said the boys were responsible for all upkeep and their own use of gasoline. The same rules applied as to the time they were to be home from a date, and the parents could interrupt any date for special errands. I don't think we'd have to worry about Jesse on any of the rules or the responsibility. He is a natural observer of rules, manners, and responsibility."

"Yes, he is all that and more," Mack agrees, "but what if he doesn't want a car just yet? Do we get him one anyway?"

"No," Joanne says. "He has to want one. I saw one for sale today that I think he'd like. It's a 1949 red Ford Deluxe. It will seat four or five people, but it is a convertible. I'm not sure I'm comfortable with him having one. What do you think?"

Before Mack can answer Jesse walks in. "Hi, Mom. Hi, Dad. What's new?"

Mack motions toward a chair and says, "Sit down for a minute, Jesse. We want to discuss something with you. Remember a few days ago we were talking about a car for you? We agreed to meet after you talked to your friends, Joanne talked to some of the mothers, and I talked to some of the fathers. Joanne and I have compared notes, and they were pretty much the same. We'd like to hear your version."

"I'd love to have a car, but after talking to guys who own one and guys who don't I've decided to wait until I graduate from high school. Most of the owners say the upkeep is expensive if you don't have a job. If you do have a job then you don't have time to study because you need to work at least part time to pay for the upkeep. The guys who don't have a car say you can get a ride with anyone who does have one, and it only takes a couple of bucks to fill the tank. The guys are grateful that they get their gas tanks filled, and you get the pleasure of riding in their cars. Now you know what to get me for graduation, don't you?"

"Yes, I guess we do," Mack says, and he reaches for his coffee cup.

Chapter 20

Tom, Joanne, and Mary are sitting in Walgreens eating their lunch. They agreed to meet today to discuss their future and becoming millionaires.

Tom says, “It’s been almost a year, and, Joanne, I haven’t heard a word about the insurance policy you were to get Mack to buy. What’s going on?”

Joanne answers, “I haven’t asked him to purchase it because he has enough insurance to set you both up for life as well as take care of Jesse and me.”

Scratching his head, Tom says, “Then what are we waiting for? Do you intend to stay married to him for the rest of your life? Have you fallen in love with him and want to renege on your promise to Mary and me? Give us some answers.”

With downcast eyes, Joanne stands up, stretches, and says, “I’m waiting for Mack to die of natural causes. I do intend to stay married to him for the rest of my life. I do love him with all my heart, and, yes, I would love to renege on my promise to you and Mary. Mack is one of the finest men I’ve ever met. He is honest, loving, compassionate, and devoted to me, Jesse, and the community. How could I ever be a part in what you and Mary want me to do? Answer me, and tell me what I owe either of you except friendship.”

Mary speaks up, “No one has asked my opinion, but you’ll get it anyway. We were kids and desperate to have a better life when we made the promise to each other. I didn’t think there would be anyone in my life except Tom. Then I met Mike. I wish he had more money because I want to spend the rest of my life with him. I want to have what Joanne’s got with Mack. I couldn’t have it unless I was willing to give up my dream, which I’m not. Yes, Mike is on his way to becoming a very rich man, but I think it will take too long, and I want the money now. Joanne, you are being very selfish to renege on your promise. That's okay, because Tom and I can continue to make plans without your knowledge and prove there is such a thing as a perfect murder. You won't know anything about it, and we'll get our money … with or without you."

"She's right, you know." Tom states. "We don't really need you, and I've become such a good friend with Mack that you can't suddenly decide not to see us anymore, can you?"

"Okay," Joanne says with a sigh. "You've made your point, and you both are blackmailers. When this is over, I never want to see either of you again. Is that understood?"

Tom jumps to his feet and rushes over to Joanne. Reaching for her, he says, "You can't mean that. Joanne, you've always been the girl for me and part of the plan was after a decent time we would marry. I can be a good stepfather to Jesse and a great husband to you … if you let me. Tell me that I'm still the man in your life. Please."

Turning from him, Joanne says, "Thoughts of a child are not necessarily the thoughts of an adult. True, back home on the mountain, you were the only man for me. That has changed. Mack has won my love and my respect. I don't think any man could make me as happy as I am with him. I definitely do not want to try to find out."

"Love is a funny thing," Mary says. "I came here to be near you, Tom, and I was sure you'd see how much I loved you, and you'd forget about Joanne and marry me. I don't want that now. I love Mike, and I sometimes wonder how I could have ever thought I loved you."

Joanne stands and says, "Tom, it looks like you'll have to find another girl to spend your millions on. I need to get home, and Mary needs to go back to work. Goodbye to both of you 'til later."

"You're right, Joanne," Mary says. "I'll talk to you later." She stands and starts walking to the bank.

"Can you pose for me Thursday afternoon?" Tom asks Joanne.

"Not this week, Tom," she answers. "I'm on the planning committee for the spring benefit the church is going to have."

"I'll see who I can get to replace you," Tom says as he walks off in a huff.

Joanne calls after him, "Good, because I don't think I'll pose for you as much as I have."

Chapter 21

Walking into the kitchen, Mack goes to Joanne, puts his arms around her and says, "Hi, Sweetheart, and how was your day?"

Turning, Joanne puts her arms around his neck, kisses him, and says, "Not too bad. I had lunch with Mary and Tom at Walgreen's and I told Tom not to count on me to pose for him as much as I have been."

"That's good," Mack remarks. "I was beginning to think there was more to your relationship than just photographer and model. That was a foolish thought, wasn't it?"

"Yes, darling, it was." Joanne answered. "I love you more everyday and there isn't any one who could replace you in my life."

"I'm glad, because I feel the same way about you. Do we have some coffee?" Mack asks as he turns from Joanne and heads for the stove.

Joanne stops him and says, "Yes, but you go sit down, and I'll bring you a cup."

After taking a drink of his coffee, he says, "I saw Tom today. I had mentioned several weeks ago that we like to camp. I even suggested that the five of us go to Natural Bridge. He told me today that he and Mary would like to go. I think it would be fun. Don't you?"

Joanne stares at Mack in disbelief, swallows, and says, "If you think so, but don't forget I'm in the middle of planning the spring benefit for the church. We'd have to make it a very short camping trip, perhaps just a day or two."

"I told him I'd let him know by Wednesday," Mack says. "That would give us both time to look at our calendars and decide when would be the best time to go. Tom would like to use us as models and make a layout of Natural Bridge. This would be a working assignment for him with us as the poster couple. I think he intends to use Mary as well. Well, what do you say?"

"I think he is conspiring to keep me as his model, and I don't like it one bit," Joanne answers with a hint of anger in her voice. "He could go camping with Mary, and they could ask another couple to go with them. Why does it have to be us?"

Looking puzzled, Mack says, "Hold on, you sound as though you don't want to be in the same room with Mary and Tom. What's going on? Is there more to your relationship than meets the eye? How about being honest with me?"

Walking over to Mack, she sits on his lap and runs her hand through his hair. "There isn't anything between Tom and me except we grew up together along with Mary. We vowed that we would all be rich when we grew up. I think Tom was sixteen, I was fourteen, and Mary was twelve. Tom, unfortunately, still has the mentality of a sixteen year old. He is good with a camera and does have a good business head but that's all."

"Honey, if he needs money, I'll see he gets a loan from the bank. In fact when I call him tomorrow about our plans, I'll bring it up, if that's okay?"

"Of course it is. Do you know how much I love you? I think you have decided to go camping with him and Mary, haven't you?"

"Yes, I think it would be fun and for added measure, we'll ask Jesse if he and some of the boys would like to go with us."

Joanne slips off Mack's lap and says, "That's a great idea. Tom will see how devoted I am to both you. Let's go look at the calendars."

Rising from the chair, Mack slips his arm around her waist and says, "Let's go."

Chapter 22

"This is great!" Jesse exclaims, "I like the log cabin and to think it sleeps eight. The guys can't wait to go hiking. Thanks for inviting us. I can't wait for tomorrow."

Laughing, Joanne says, "You'll have to because it'll be dark in a few minutes and I, for one, don't want to look for you and your friends in the dark. I don't think the bears are too friendly. Okay?"

Mack winks at her and tells his son, "I don't know, we've been trying to get rid of him since the honeymoon. Maybe he should go hiking now. An accident could happen, and we'd be rid of the problem."

Joanne shudders and Mack hurries over to her. "Honey what's wrong? Are you coming down with something? Let me get you a sweater, and I'll go to the lodge and get something to eat for supper. I want you to rest. Jesse, get me a blanket."

Putting the blanket around Joanne, Mack tells her, "I'll be right back. Jesse, you and the boys stay with her. We'll eat as soon as I get back, okay?"

"Honestly, Mack," Joanne states, "I'm fine. It's like my mother used to say, 'Someone just walked over my grave'."

"What a horrible thought," Jesse says. "Sure, Dad, we won't leave her side until you come back with the food. When will Tom and Mary get here?"

"Any time. I'll get enough food for them," Mack answers as he walks out the door.

***

Mary looks at Tom and says, "I had plans to go away this weekend with Mike, not with you."

Tom answers, "You do want your share of the fortune when Mack dies, don't you? This is the perfect setup for the PERFECT murder. We'll go hiking, and you girls will go ahead while Mack and I hang back. I'll have my camera, and when we get to a pinnacle that's tall enough, I'll have him pose with the view in the back and on both sides of him. Only, I'll have him back up until he falls. How does that sound?"

"I ... I don't know," Mary stammers. "It might work ... then again it might not. Did Joanne approve this plan?"

"No, she didn't, and I don't intend to let her know of the plan. She'd cancel the trip and never speak to either of us again. She thinks she's in love with him."

Mary stares at Tom and says, "She is in love with both Mack and Jesse. I'm willing to forget our childhood dreams if you are. I just want all of us to be happy. You could find another girl, fall in love, get married, and have a dozen kids. I have quite a bit of money saved, and so has Mike. I don't think either of us will suffer financially if we married within the next four or five months. I bet you have quite a tidy sum saved also. Don't you?"

Tom glances at her and answers, "Yes, I do, but not as much as I'd have if Mack died and Joanne kept her end of the bargain. I'm in love with her, and I intend to marry her when Mack dies."

Mary gasps and asks, "How do you know she'll still want you?"

Turning steely eyes to Mary, Tom says, "I'll make sure she marries me. She wouldn't want to be accused of being an accessory to murder, would she?"

"This is a side of you I don't know." Mary says, "I'm not sure I want to know you anymore. Help me understand why you're going to force her to marry you. Don't you want her to be happy?"

"We'll have to continue this conversation some other time," Tom says as he drives the car into the driveway of the cabin.

Jesse rushes to the car and says, "I'm starving, and Dad has gone to pick up our supper. I'll give you a hand with the suitcases."

Laughing, Tom gets out of the car. "That sounds like a plan to me." He walks around and opens the car door for Mary.

"Hi, Jesse," Marysays. "How's it going?"

Bubbling over with enthusiasm, Jess answers, "Fine. I brought a couple of buddies with me, and we're having the time of our lives. Now that you're here, we won't have to entertain Dad and Mom, and we can do our own thing."

Before Mary can answer, Tom says, "Sounds good. I want to take some photos of your dad climbing the trails and maybe a few of Joanne. Mostly, I want a lot of scenery photos. Did you bring your camera?"

Jesse answers, "Yes, I did, and I think I'll try to make a travel log with just a few words and a lot of pictures. How does that sound?"

Tom says, "Sounds to me like you want to combine your photos and a story in one book."

"I do, and I hope you'll help me with the pictures." Jesse says, as he takes a couple of suitcases from the trunk of the car.

Chapter 23

Mack has put the bacon on the grill, the eggs in the skillet, and the biscuits in the oven. He let everyone sleep, but breakfast is almost ready. He takes a pan out of the cabinet and a spoon from the drawer. He walks up and down the hall to the bedrooms banging the spoon against the pan. Jesse is the first person to respond.

"What is going on?" Jesse demands as he stretches and rubs his eyes.

With a mischievous grin and a twinkle in his eyes, Mack says, "Breakfast is ready, the sun is almost up, and I want to get an early start on the trails."

Joanne opens the door to their bedroom, yawns, and says, "You didn't tell me we were getting up before the rooster crowed."

Going over to his wife, he kisses her and tells her, "Good morning, Love. It's going to be a beautiful day, and I want to share it all with you. Now get dressed, and come to breakfast."

"Okay," Joanne says. "I'll wake Mary, and we'll be there shortly."

Jesse turns to go back into his bedroom when his two friends appear already dressed. Jim says, "Good morning, everyone. I'm ready to go explore the world. Anyone with me or do you all need to take your daily supplement of energy this morning?"

They both say, "Yes, we do."

Laughing, Jim says, "Yes, you do what?"

Joanne answers, "We are old folks, and we need our daily supply of food. Can't live without it."

They all laugh.

Jim says, "I'm ready. I'll come with you, Mr. Stevens and help in the kitchen."

"That would be a big help." Mack says as he and Jim walk to the kitchen.

Joanne starts for the bedroom when Tom appears and says, “Today is the first day of our lives together.”

Joanne stares at him. After several seconds she tells him, “Don’t you dare harm a hair on his head. If you do, you’ll have me to deal with. I’ve told you that I love him, and Jesse is a delight to be around. My life is perfect, and if you really loved me, you’d be happy for me. When Mack dies of natural causes, I’ll honor my agreement with you and Mary but not before. Do you understand me?”

“Hey, hold on a minute,” Tom tells her. “I can’t help it if there is some loose dirt, and he gets too close to the edge, now can I?”

“Let’s just hope that doesn’t happen, okay?” and Joanne turns and walks into the bedroom.

***

“Okay, boys,” Mack calls to them, “here are the ground rules. Number 1: Make sure you do not get separated from each other. Number 2: Do not go exploring beyond the paths. Number 3: Don’t get to close to the edge, and, last but not least, Jesse, please do not take unnecessary chances just for a great picture. Go and have fun. We’ll meet back here about 4:00. Okay? Make sure you have your lunches packed.”

“Sure, Dad,” Jesse says, and then with a twinkle in his eye he adds, “However, with your rules, I’m not sure we can have any fun. What’s a hike without risks? I may see a bear with a cub and maybe, just maybe, the only good shot would be the tree branch hanging over them. Couldn’t I climb the tree, just this once?”

Laughing, Mack tells him, “Go on and have a SAFE, fun filled day. See you at 4:00.”

The boys head out and are discussing which trail to take when Joanne approaches Mack’s side. “We’re already to go. I’ve divided the lunches up among the backpacks. I can’t wait to see the scenery.”

“Good,” Mack says, “because I’ve wanted to come here for a long time. Joanne, I’m so glad you married me. You have been a blessing to both Jesse and me. I love you so much.”

“I love you too,” Joanne answers, and she gives him a kiss on the cheek.

Chapter 24

Sitting on the ground and finishing their sandwiches, Mack asks, "I wonder how the boys are doing?"

Wiping her mouth, Joanne answers, "I'm sure they are fine. Otherwise, we would have heard from them by now."

"Definitely," Tom says. "We told them which trail we were taking, and they told us theirs also. I don't think we have to worry about them at all."

Scratching his head, Mack says, "You're right, of course. However, I know what the dangers are, and boys sometimes get too eager to explore something without thinking of what could happen."

"Not Jesse," Joanne tells them. "He is one of the most level headed boys I know. He'll keep the others from getting into trouble. Anyway, I'm ready to start again. It is so beautiful here that I can't wait to see what the next scene will be."

They all rise and start up the trail again.

***

"Come on, Jesse, grow up." Jimmy taunts, "Just 'cause your dad told us not to go exploring, doesn't mean we have to do exactly what he tells us. Does it?"

Puffing up his chest and pointing a finger at Jim, Jesse answers, "Yes, because I would have drowned if Dad and Joanne weren't with me in the Smokys. The land and the rocks in the mountains can be deceiving. I thought the rock in the creek was close to the top of the stream. It wasn't, and I went down to my neck instead of the bottom of my shoe. The rocks are home to all kinds of snakes, and some of them are poisonous. There are covered holes that we could fall into, and there are chasms that are deceiving. We're not sure how long it would take to locate someone to help us out. We can ask Dad and Tom to go with us while the ladies do something else if you'd like."

"That sounds a lot better than always staying on the trail." Jimmy says, reluctantly.

The boys start up the trail again with Jesse in the lead.

***

"Oh, look at this!" Joanne exclaims. "I think I'm standing on the edge of the world. The tops of the trees in the valley are so close together. They look like a lush green carpet. You can see a slight clearing where the farm house and the barn are sitting. Wonder how much land he has. It doesn't look like more than a postage stamp."

Mary puts her hands on her hips and says, "I swear, Joanne, I'd thought you'd be so tired of this kind of scenery. It's almost like the mountains where we grew up."

Walking over to Mary, Joanne puts a hand on her shoulder and tells her, "Yes, it is, and I never got tired of looking down from our mountain tops. Every day the scenery changed. It wasn't very noticeable, but it did change. Sometimes it would be a tree branch that looked out of place until you realized that the wind had taken the limb next to it and thrown it to the ground. In the spring you could see the wild flowers, and sometimes the wild grapes were in bloom. I loved walking up the mountain and eating the grapes."

"Yes," Tom joins in, "I always enjoyed swinging on the grape vine and dropping into the old swimming hole."

"You both sound like you're homesick," Mary says. "I, for one, don't care if I ever see another mountain in my lifetime. I thought there would be something different about this mountain ... but you see one mountain, you've seen them all."

Mack looks from one to the other and says, "I can't wait for Joanne to invite me to see her mountain and her home."

Laughing, Joanne walks over to him, kisses him on the cheek and says, "I want to wait until I'm sure you won't run away when you see my humble beginnings."

Circling his arm around her waist, he tells her, "You don't have to worry. Nothing could take me away from you. I'm afraid Jesse wouldn't speak to me for the rest of my life if I left."

"Good," Joanne says and starts up the trail.

"This is such a good spot, Mack," Tom says, "let's let the girls go on ahead while I take a few shots of you with the valley in the background."

"Okay," Mack tells him and walks to the edge of the mountain.

"That's perfect, Mack. Now if you can back up just a little more, turn a little sideways, and put your hand on your chin. I want to show you really studying the landscape."

Mack looks around and spots a large boulder. He walks toward it and says, "How about I sit on the top of this rock and look at the scenery?"

"I think that would be perfect. Then I want one of you as close to the edge as you can get."

Laughing Mack says, "It's a good thing I'm not afraid of heights, or we'd both be in trouble. I'd probably fall over the cliff, and you'd be accused of pushing me."

Tom laughs and tells him, "You're right, but since you're a daredevil, I don't have to worry, do I?"

"No, you don't," and Mack walks to the very edge.

There is a very piercing scream and both Mack and Tom start running in the direction of the girls. Reaching them, they see Mary on the ground and Joanne stooping beside her.

Mack is the first to reach them and he says, "What happened? Where is the first aid kit?"

Joanne answers, "She saw a snake and panicked. She turned her ankle when she started to run. I've given her an aspirin and I'll wrap her ankle to keep the swelling down. Maybe we should put a couple of twigs on either side of the ankle so it can't move. Just in case it's broken."

Tom speaks up, "I hope she was running to me instead of the other way."

Mary with tears running down her cheeks says, "Hey, guys, I'm in a lot of pain. How am I going to get down from this oversized hill?"

"I think Tom and I can carry you in an arm chair. I'm not sure Joanne can handle all the backpacks."

"Mack," Tom says, "I think I can carry my backpack and still hold up my half of the chair for Mary. Do you think you can handle your backpack?"

Mack scratches his head and thoughtfully says, "First, let's go through all the backpacks and see what we can throw away. I know that will take up time, but we want to get her back down the trail as soon as possible, and with less weight on our backs we can carry her more easily."

"You're right. Let's start with Mary's and Joanne's as we'll have to combine the two into one," Tom says.

Joanne starts emptying both backpacks. Tom and Mack join her, and between them they have the backpacks combined into one. Next they start on Tom's and Mack's.

"Finally, we're ready for the arm chair." Mack says, "How are you feeling, Mary?"

"Not much better, but I'll make it. Are you sure you can handle me and your backpacks?"

Mack laughs and says, "Sure we can. Joanne will help you into our chair, and if we get tired, you might land on your head. That's one sure way of forgetting about your ankle."

Exasperated, Mary retorts, "Laugh, but you drop me, and I'll get even with poison in your coffee. Now, slaves, to the castle."

Tom looks at Mack and says, "I'm sorry, but it has been a long time since I made an arm chair. Tell me what to do."

"Okay." Mack answers. "Take your right hand and put it on your left elbow. I'll do the same with my right hand. That leaves your right arm extended and my right arm extended. We walk towards each other, and your extended hand takes hold of my bent arm. My extended hand takes hold of your bent arm. Mary will sit on the four arms with one arm around each of our necks. Are we ready?"

"Yes," they all say.

Tom and Mack bend down at their knees while keeping their arms steady. Joanne helps Mary up while keeping her weight off the injured ankle. Together they get Mary in the chair, and the boys stand up together. Mack says, "That went smoothly. I pray we get down the mountain as easily."

"No matter what," Tom says, "we'll succeed, and I don't want to volunteer for another rescue mission, so everyone watch your Ps and Qs, okay?"

Joanne can't help it; she starts to giggle, "Tom, you watch yourself. It's been a long time since you roamed the mountains at home."

Mary groans, "Please all of you just get me to a doctor. I'm hurting and worried that one of you guys will stumble, and there I'll go head over foot all the way down."

"Not if we can help it." Mack tells her.

***

"I've got to stop and rest," Mack says. "My arms feel as though someone has shot them and then refused to help."

"Me too," Tom says.

Joanne stops and puts the backpack on the ground. She walks over to the men and helps Mary out of the arm chair and to a rock.

They don't sit very long when they hear their names being called. "I wonder what's wrong now," Mack says, as he looks in the direction of the voices. "It sounds like Jesse."

Rounding the corner of the trail, Jesse sees his dad and the others. "We got back to the cabin early and decided to try to catch up with you. Is this as far as you got?"

"No, Jesse, it isn't," Mack answers. "Mary hurt her ankle, and we stopped here for our second wind before proceeding down to the cabin."

Tim speaks up, "It's a good thing we came to find you. We can make an arm chair or we can carry the backpacks. Whichever you'd rather have us do."

Mack shakes his head and says, "Boys we're glad to see you, and, yes, two of you can make the arm chair and the other one can take Joanne's backpack. By the way, how much further is it to the cabin?"

"Not far," Jesse answers. "We didn't want to help for a long distance, so we waited until we thought you would be so grateful that you'd suspend those rules about the trail." He gives a small laugh.

"We'll talk about it," Mack says as he rises to his feet.

***

"Thank goodness it isn't broken," Mary says. "It's just a bad sprain. The doctor said I wasn't to travel for a couple of days. So, how about you and Mack taking the boys on a hike tomorrow while Joanne and I sit here and play games?"

Tom shakes his head and says, "I don't know. I think we should get you back home as quickly as possible. We can come back another time. Wouldn't you and Joanne get bored just sitting here in the cabin?"

"I wouldn't because the pain pills will make me sleep. We'll have to ask Joanne how she feels about it."

Walking into the kitchen, Tom picks up a cup and pours himself some coffee. He sits down at the table and says, "Well, are we going to leave tomorrow morning or let Mary rest another day before heading home?"

Mack says, "Actually, I was thinking of staying until Tuesday. Mary could rest for two whole days and the boys, with you and me, could do some exploring. Joanne and I discussed it, and she is willing to nurse Mary."

"It sounds like a great idea, but wouldn't Joanne get bored?"

Mack gives a small laugh, "You don't know how resourceful my wife can be, do you? She can find the most fascinating things to do with her time. I've been very blessed to have found her and for her to love me."

Tom takes a sip of his coffee and asks, "Where is she? We should ask her how she feels about it."

"I did, and she was the one who made the suggestion that we stay. She had already called Mary's assistant and asked her to call us Monday morning so I could give her instructions on the daily work. Joanne is truly remarkable."

Tom agrees, "Yes, she is, but you didn't answer my question. Where is she?"

"As usual, she is in control. She went down to the lodge to make arrangements for someone to come and help Mary out on the porch tomorrow afternoon. Joanne also went to purchase some books and magazines. We brought a lot of board games. I don't think either girl is going to miss us or get bored."

A car pulls into the driveway and Tom looks at Mack and asks, "Who could that be?"

Before Mack can answer, the door opens and in walks Joanne with her arms loaded with groceries and books. Behind her is the lodge manager pushing a wheelchair. Tom rushes over and takes the groceries from her and says, "Looks like we are staying for awhile, whether we want to or not."

Joanne laughs and answers, "Yes, we are and it's all your fault, Tom. She was wondering where you two were and she wasn't watching the trail. She saw the snake but she didn't see the rock jutting out of the path and tripped over it. When she fell, that's when her ankle doubled under her."

In a huff, Tom explains, "I didn't get the shot of Mack I wanted, because she screamed just as I was about to pose Mack."

Joanne becomes very serious and says, "I guess you weren't

supposed to take that shot. God was looking out for all of us. I think it's meant for us to stay another day or two."

Mack walks over to Joanne and gives her a kiss on the cheek. "Honey, it's been a long day, and tomorrow will be even longer. I think we'd better think of going to bed."

"I am tired, but I want to check on Mary first. Then I'll be right in."

Chapter 25

Entering the bedroom, Joanne asks, “Honey, are you asleep?”

Turning over, Mack answers, “No I’m not. Is everything okay?”

“I’m not sure. Mary was sound asleep but she must have been dreaming because she was moaning. The sound was so disturbing that I almost woke her.”

“She is in pain, and the pain pills are making her sleep, but the pain is still in her subconscious. The moans you heard are the result of her brain telling the world that she hurts.”

“You’re probably right. I’m sure she’ll be better in the morning. Under her breath, she says, “I hope.”

Mack watches Joanne as she walks over to the bed and says, “While we’re on the subject of Mary, I don’t think Tom is in love with her.”

“Oh, what makes you think that?”

“Joanne, he watches you all the time. When you come in the room, he practically glows. It’s as if he lives to be near you.”

“Don’t be ridiculous!” Joanne exclaims. “I’ve known Tom and Mary all my life, and he sure would have let me know before now,if he felt anything but friendship towards me.”

Reaching for his wife, Mack says, “I don’t think he knew it until you married me. The thought of my money triggered his greed, and I think Mary falling was God’s way of protecting me.”

“Wh ... what do you mean?” Joanne asks as she throws her hand to her mouth.

“I mean, I think I was the one that was intended to have an accident. Tom certainly kept moving me closer to the edge of the cliff. I was backing up and couldn’t see how close I was coming to the edge. Since the accident, I’ve had a lot of time to think and I’m sure I need to watch my step around him. Maybe we should step away from his friendship and you should quit posing for him altogether. What do you think?”

“I think you’re imagining things that don’t exist. If I thought he might harm you or Jesse I’d never let him near either one of you. Anyway, Tom and Mary have been friends all of their lives and they fell in love during their teens. As for me quitting, maybe I will cut back some more but only because I need to become more involved with the school. Jesse will be graduating in a few years. I would like to become an adult advisor for his class.”

“No, Honey, that won’t do,” Mack says. “You need to quit completely. Otherwise, Tom will always try to come between us, and I’m sure you wouldn’t want to hurt Mary.”

“I’ll give it some thought. I’m tired and I want to go to sleep. So here’s your goodnight kiss,” she says and kisses him on the lips.

Mack tightens his arm around her and whispers, “Good night, Love. I don’t think I could live if I lost you.”

***

Joanne is fixing a tray for Mary when Tom walks into the kitchen. “Good morning, Tom,” she says. “I’m taking a tray in to Mary, or would you like to take it?”

“Sure, I’ll take it. Maybe I should run outside and find a wild flower to put on it.”

Joanne laughs and says, “I’m afraid the food would be cold before you returned. You’d get so involved in looking at the scenery that you’d forget what you were supposed to do.”

Tom picks up the tray, sticks his tongue out at Joanne, and says, “You may be right, but I don’t forget the important things in my life,” and he walks out the door.

Mack walks in and takes Joanne in his arms. “Good morning, Love. Did you sleep well?”

Joanne kisses him on the cheek and answers, “Yes, I did. I think the excitement was a little too much for me yesterday. I was so exhausted, couldn’t wait to go to sleep.”

“I know, I started to ask you something and realized that you were already asleep. Anyway, after the boys have eaten, I think Tom and I will take them on an exploration of the mountain. Do you think you can entertain yourself and Mary for the rest of the day?”

Joanne tells him, “Let’s eat and then you and Tom can take the boys exploring. When I went to the lodge last night I picked up some of the books from their library. We brought some magazines, and with the board games, we should be set for the day."

"I can do that," Mack says. "Take your time. I'm sure the boys won't be up for awhile."

"You're wrong, Dad," Jesse says as he walks into the kitchen.

"Aha!" Mack states, "You're the only one I see, and you'll have to wait on Tim and Jim to go anywhere. Joanne and I haven't had breakfast yet."

Joanne sets a plate of toast, eggs, and bacon in front of Mack. She then sets a plate in front of Jesse and takes one for herself. She sits down and asks, "Are we ready to eat? Mack will you say our morning prayer?"

Mack answers, "Yes." With bowed head he says, "Our Heavenly Father, thank you for the food we are about to partake of. Please help it to nourish our bodies and our souls. Help us to enjoy Your beautiful mountain and keep us from all harm. I ask this in Jesus' name. Not my will, but Yours, be done. Amen."

Joanne tells them as she rises from the table, "I don't want to keep you from your mountain climbing. So, if you don't mind, I'll let you clean the kitchen and feed the rest while I go see to Mary."

"Be on your way," Mack answers. "We'll do fine without you hovering over us like an old wet hen."

Joanne laughs and walks over to Mack, kisses him on the lips, and says, "I'll need to go to the lodge to see if they have a pair of white gloves. I'll have to check your housekeeping, and I can't do a decent job without the gloves."

Mack and Jesse look at one another. Mack says, "Believe me, Sergeant, we'll do a great job." Then he salutes her.

They all laugh and Joanne leaves the room.

***

Jesse is the first one back to the cabin. He runs into Joanne, and with excitement in his voice says, "We had a great time! You should have been with us. Remember on your honeymoon how Dad and you teased me about throwing me off a cliff?" Without waiting for an answer, he continues, "Well, you should have had your honeymoon here. There are great sights and a lot of the trails don't have rails, so you can leave the trail and strike out on your own. Dad's right, nobody should leave these trails without having someone with you ... or two or more. Anyway, Mom, we did some exploring and discovered several bears. There was one with two babies. I took lots and lots of pictures. I think Tom took some also, but he and dad were in a serious conversation, and I don't think they even noticed that we had ventured ahead of them on our own. You should see the Natural Bridge. I couldn't believe it. A great big red rock extending from one mountain to another with nothing, I mean absolutely nothing, underneath it. We walked on it, and the scenery was spectacular. I can't wait to see that picture."

"Boy!" exclaims Mack as he walks over to Joanne and kisses her. "What a day! Joanne, I wish you were there. We saw all kinds of animals, and, if we were quiet, they ignored us like we were a tree or something. We saw them play, stop, sniff the air, and take off in a run. We let the boys explore, and they didn't get into trouble. The bridge is very impressive. I can't wait to see Jesse's photos. I think he took six rolls of film. Didn't you, son?"

"Not quite, Dad," Jesse answers, "but close. I took five and started on the sixth. I'm sure glad I brought 10 rolls. I didn't want to run out but if we stay another day, I know I will."

Laughing, Joanne says, "I'm glad you both had a good time, but did the others enjoy themselves?"

They all agree, "We sure did."

Tim says, "Jesse and Mr. Stevens have told you everything we did. We have to find a new audience so we can tell our version. Don't we, Tom?"

Chuckling and clapping Tim on the back, Tom answers, "Yes, we will. I got some very good shots of the boys, the scenery, and of Mack. After the photos are developed, I'll let you have your pick. The boys can take the ones they like also." Holding up his hand in a stop motion, he continues, "I know what you are going to say, Joanne, and I have that covered. I've already had each and every one sign releases so I can sell the photos to a magazine. I'm going to write a cover story to go with the pictures."

"That sounds great," Joanne tells him. "Now, we do need supper. I wasn't sure what time you'd get back so I haven't even started. Mack, do you want me to cook, or will you and Tom go to the Lodge and get us something to eat?"

Mack looks at Tom and says, "I don't think we could eat a thing. We're too excited to even think of food."

Jesse stomps his foot and exclaims, "We're never too excited or tired to pass up a meal, snack, or anything else that involves food. If you guys are too tired and excited to go, we'll go. Just be warned that we may bring back all junk food."

Laughing, Mack walks over to Jesse and puts an arm around his shoulders. "Son, do you think I'll let you get even with me for our honeymoon? Well, I won't. You and the boys can go with us to the lodge as we'll need someone to carry the supper back."

Jim speaks up and says, "I thought this would be a fun trip without any responsibilities. Now, I discover I have to act like a pack horse and carry food from the lodge to here. I'm too young to be treated this way."

They all laugh, and Mack says, "Come, mules, we can't have the ladies starving to death ... can we?"

"No," the boys say as they all walk out the door.

Chapter 26

Mary is sitting at a table in Central Park when Tom approaches. “Good afternoon, Mary. How is the ankle?”

She smiles and answers, “Fine. Wasn’t the weekend fun? I know I had fun even with the accident.”

“Sure, it was fun,” Tom says as he sits across from her. “If it hadn’t been for your screaming, we’d be on our way to being millionaires. I had Mack just one step from going over that cliff.”

Looking at Tom with daggers in her eyes Mary says, “I think Joanne really loves the guy, her step-son, and her life. If you do succeed in killing Mack, I don’t think she’ll marry you.”

Pouting and looking at the street, Tom tells her, “She promised, and you know we don’t go back on our promises to each other.”

Exasperated, Mary throws her hands up in the air and says, “We were kids then. We’re adults now. Promises made as children are made to be broken, and I’ll not help you in your scheme either.”

“Oh, yes, you will.”

“What will you do? Tell Mack his life is in danger by you?”

“I’ll do better than that,” Tom retorts. “I’ll tell him that Joanne wanted to pay me $500,000 dollars to kill him.”

Mary looks at him with daggers in her eyes. “You wouldn’t do that!”

“Back out and watch me destroy her marriage.”

Softly crying, Mary sits down again and puts her head in her arms. “Okay, you win.”

Mike walks up and takes in the scene. “What’s going on here?” he demands.

Mary rises, wipes her eyes, and walks to him, “Nothing, Love, we were having a little disagreement, and I got angry.”

Looking at Tom and taking Mary in his arms, Mike says, “Tom talks in his sleep. So I think I know what this is about. Looks like

God is watching over Mack and Joanne. I think I'd watch what I do, if I was you, Tom."

Laughing, Tom says, "Are you going to play big brother now and tell on me?"

"No," Mike says as he turns away from Mary, "but I will tell if you do anything to harm Mack Stevens."

"That's a form of blackmail."

"I know," Mike says. "You'd better hope nothing happens to him while you're with him."

Rising, Mary says, "I've got to go back to work. So I'll say goodbye for now."

Mike kisses her and says, "I'll see you tonight about 8:00, okay?"

She walks away, turning to answer, "Yes, Dear."

"Now, Tom, about this plan to get millions without working for it. Prison isn't a nice place to be. There are men who will cut your throat for a dime and lie about who did it. They have gangs in there, and you don't dare cross them. I don't think for one minute that you'd survive one night. I had the respect of them because I was the driver for the moonshiners. Most of them hired others to drive for them. I was offered all kinds of driving jobs on the outside ... all illegal. I'm so lucky to have found a job driving for the On Time Trucking Company. Don't mess it up for all of us. I mean it."

"I don't intend to," Tom answers, glaring at Mike. "I can't help it if an accident happens and Mack gets killed, can I?"

"You'll never get Joanne to believe it was an accident," Mike says. "She loves the guy, and she knows what you are planning to do. I think you'd better forget it and wait patiently until he dies of natural causes. Now you have three people who know what you want to do ... me, Mary, and Joanne. All who could blackmail you out of your millions down the road."

Tom scratches his head and thoughtfully says, "Neither girl would do that to me. You, on the other hand, might."

"Don't be ridiculous!" Mike exclaims. "I wouldn't do that to my worst enemy. However, I don't want to marry Mary under those circumstances. It would always be over our heads and eventually would drive us apart. If she could be a part of this scheme, maybe in the future, I'd become the victim."

"I don't think you have to worry," Tom says. "Mary is ready to marry you, with or without money, and she wants to quit also."

"Good," Mike stands up. "I'll talk to her tonight. Anyway, I've got to go. Think about what I said. I hope you decide to drop this crazy scheme of yours."

***

Looking at Mary with love in his eyes, Mike asks, "Where would you like to go tonight?"

"How about boarding the Belle of Louisville?" Mary asks as she kisses him on the cheek.

"That's just what the doctor ordered. We'd have privacy and a slow boat to enjoy the stars and moon."

Mary laughs and says, "I'm not so sure of the privacy part. Tonight they have a band for dancing, and the cruise doesn't start until 9:30. I thought we could grab a sandwich on the way to the boat."

"It'll have to be a quick bite," Mike says as he kisses her. "Let's go to Kingfish. It's close to the landing, and the fish is great."

"Okay," Mary says as she reaches for the door.

***

Walking hand in hand, Mike and Mary are silent. They are enjoying the evening and each other's company. Suddenly, Mike stops, turns, and takes Mary in his arms. He kisses her and stepping back, he says, "Mary, I have quite a bit of money saved, and I want you to set the date for our wedding."

"Oh Mike, I'd love to, but you know I'm committed to the vow I made with Tom and Joanne when we were kids."

"Look," Mike says, "we all do foolish things when we're children, but they are forgotten, and life goes on. That wasn't a foolish vow, but the way Tom is thinking about it makes it one now. He could cause both you and Joanne your happiness, and if he was caught, he'd name you both as his accomplices. Joanne would lose her marriage and her life, and I wouldn't get to marry you. Is this scheme of Tom's worth it?"

Mary sighs, looks at Mike, and tells him, "When you put it that way, NO, it isn't. Tom is blackmailing us into helping him. He threatens to tell Mack, and you know what that would do to Joanne's marriage and my job. We don't know what to do except to keep praying."

Taking her hand and stating to walk again, Mike says, "Maybe

I can help."

Mike becomes silent as he tries to think of a way he could help and not get caught.

Chapter 27

Mike calls the On Time Trucking Firm and says, "I'm sorry but I must have ate something that didn't agree with me last night. I can't stay out of the bathroom. If I'm not better by this afternoon, I'm going to call the doctor. I won't be in today but hopefully I'll be in tomorrow."

His boss tells him, "We'll have a load for you in the morning. Get well and we'll see you tomorrow."

As soon as he hangs up the phone he starts for the door. He stops, scratches his head, and thinks *I think I have everything I need except I don't know what kind of car Mack drives or where he parks it. I hate to involve Mary but I'll have to get the information from her.*

Mary is startled to hear Mike's voice on the phone but tries to act normal.

Mary pleads as she twists her hair. "Oh Mike please don't get involved.

"Oh okay. He drives a blue Buick. It's a 1952 Special Riviera. There is a parking lot on 5th Street and he usually parks about the third row in. Be careful I love you." She hangs up the phone.

***

Mike hangs up the phone and walks to the window. He scratches his head and thinks *I must be crazy. I'm risking my life and my future to fulfill a dumb commitment Mary made with Tom when she was a kid. The only thing I know for sure is she'll keep up the charade of being in love with Tom until the scheme is fulfilled. Enough of this I'll just do what I have to do. I'll go to the lot and tell the attendant that Mr. Stevens told me he was having a slight problem with the car and would I check it out. I'll take it out to a secluded spot and cut the guide wire in the steering column not all the way but just enough to cause it to break after he starts home tonight. Then everyone will be happy and they'll all think it's an accident. I want to marry Mary enough to take a chance.* He walks out the door.

***

"Mary," Mack says as he walks from his office, "please type these letters before you go home. I'll see you tomorrow."

"Okay, and please be safe. Tell Joanne to call me when she has a chance."

"Will do." Mack answers, and he leaves the office.

He enters the parking lot, and the attendant hands him his keys, saying, "I didn't know you were having trouble with your car."

Startled, Mack says, "I'm not; why do you think I am?"

Scratching his head the attendant says, "Well, a mechanic came this morning and took your car for a test drive. He said he couldn't find anything wrong with it, and he would tell you himself."

"You're right. I did call a friend and ask him to check the car. I forgot for a minute. Thanks. I'll see you tomorrow."

As Mack walks to the car he thinks, *I'd better have the car checked before I start home. There is a garage on Broadway. I'll stop there.*

The manager of the garage says, "It'll be a few minutes, but it shouldn't take more than an hour to check all the wires and the brakes."

"Thanks. I'll be in the waiting room." Mack enters the room and notices that he is the only one there. He goes to the pay phone and calls Joanne to tell her he is detained. He doesn't tell her why. Hanging up the phone he wonders, *Is someone out to kill me? I'll have to be careful and listen to all conversations. I know Joanne or Jesse can't be involved, but I wouldn't put it past Tom. He doesn't even try to disguise his feelings for my wife. Maybe I should run a background check on him. That's what I'll do first thing in the morning, and I won't let Mary know about it.*

The manager enters the waiting room and hands Mack his car keys and the bill. He says, "I've never seen the steering wire break in quite this way. Anyway, we replaced it. We couldn't find anything else wrong."

Mack answers, “Thanks. I'll see you later.” He pays the bill and drives home.

Chapter 28

Jesse, Tim, and Jim are standing in the hall at school when Mr. O'Brien approaches. "Boys, I'm thinking of starting a new extracurricular activity and wonder if your fathers would like to participate."

Jesse is the first to speak, "What is it, and why do you think we would be interested?"

"I have put my suggestion before the school board and will have my answer in a few days. I feel that it is a great idea, and I'm prepared to share it with you and your fathers."

"So?" Tim asks.

"Yeah," Jim says, "we were just saying we think we're too old to be hanging out with our fathers, and you come along with this. What is your idea?"

Scratching his head, Mr. O'Brien tells them, "I want to start a flying club. We'd meet at the airport and learn how to fly a plane. I think it would be a good idea to involve your fathers because then you'd always have someone to fly with. What do you think?"

Stunned and with a slow recovery, Jesse says, "I'm in. When do we start? I could start this Saturday. Dad hasn't come up with anything to do this weekend. How many will be in the club, and will we work on getting our wings?"

Laughing, Mr. O'Brien says, "Hold on. The board hasn't said we can do this, and I don't want to go against their wishes."

Jim asks, "When do they meet to make their decision?"

Mr. O'Brien tells them, "They'll meet this Thursday night at the airport with me."

Jesse turns to the other boys and says, "Maybe we could get our dads to meet them at the same time." After some thought he says, "We do need more information to give to 'em."

"Yes, boys, you do. If you will come with me, I'll give you literature to take home. This club will teach you about airplanes.

It'll prepare you for a career in aerodynamics, if you'd be interested."

Excited, Tim exclaims, "I haven't told anyone, but I want to be an astronaut! This would be the first step. I'll call Dad at lunch and have an answer for you this afternoon. Wow! My dream is within reach!"

Jim laughs and says, "Tim, you sound like the girls when they get excited."

Blushing, Tim tells him, "I bet you'd act the same way if your dream was an impossible dream, and someone handed you the opportunity to reach for it."

Mr. O'Brien clears his throat and says, "Let's proceed to my room for the brochures, okay?"

Excitedly, they say, "Okay."

***

Rushing into the house, Jesse calls, "Mom, Mom, where are you? Mom, I need to talk to you."

"Here I am," Joanne says as she walks into the hall. "What is all the excitement? Are you hurt?"

"I'm okay, Mom, but I have some exciting news, and I want you to help me convince Dad that this is good for me."

Laughing and taking Jesse into her arms, she says, "I can't very well convince Mack of anything if I don't know what it is, can I?"

"I'm sorry," Jesse says as he turns away from Joanne. "One of the teachers, Mr. O'Brien, stopped me, Jim, and Tim in the hall at school today. He wants to start a flying club. We'd meet every Saturday morning at the airport to study aviation and eventually learn to fly. Tim wants to become an astronaut, and this is a golden opportunity for him. I just want to fly. Who knows, when I'm rich and famous, I could own my own plane and fly all over the world. I have some brochures telling about the airport, what would be expected of me as a student, and what the airport's obligation would be. Please help me. Please."

"Give me a few minutes to study the brochures, and then I'll discuss it with you." Joanne reaches for the pamphlets.

Jesse hands them to her and says, "I'll go to my room. When you've finished, call me, and I'll come down."

"Okay," Joanne says, and she heads for the kitchen.

After a few minutes, Joanne calls Jesse. "Come on down. I've made you a cup of hot chocolate and also cut you a piece of pie."

Entering the kitchen, Jesse asks, "Do you think Dad will approve of this project? What do you think of it?"

Joanne pours herself a cup of coffee and sits opposite Jesse at the table. "You know, Jess, that the questions I'm going to ask will be about the same ones your dad will ask, don't you?"

Hanging his head, Jesse answers, "Yes, that's why I asked for your help."

"Okay, here we go." Joanne then takes a pad and a pencil and asks, "Question number one: Do you want to do this or do you just want to be with your friends? If they decide to quit, will you quit also, or will you stay with the program?"

Laughing, Jesse says, "No fair! That's two questions! Anyway, I want to do it. I think it is something that will look good on my application for college. I really don't care what Tim and Jim do. I intend to learn to fly and receive my wings. I may even decide to make flying my career. I understand the Army has a great air force, and the commercial pilots make a lot of money besides seeing all the exotic places in the world."

Joanne shakes her head and asks, "Did you read the brochures and discuss with your teacher and the boys what your answers would be?"

"Honestly, Mom, we didn't have time to discuss anything after we picked up the pamphlets because we had to get to class. I rushed home so we could talk about it before Dad got home."

"It says there may be a time when you would be called to help in the control tower or fly somewhere on an emergency flight. How would you feel if you were called and you had a date with the most popular girl in school?"

"Really, Mom, I wouldn't like it, and you know I wouldn't like it. but because this is what I want to do, I've promised to be available at all times. After I've had training, I'd go without a word."

"What about the girl and her feelings?"

"I guess she'd have to accept my job. Mom, this may be a volunteer position, but it will be part of my life, and any girl would have to understand. I'm sorry, but if she didn't then she isn't the girl I thought she was, and we would break up."

Joanne sighs and asks the last question, "If the United States would go to war and you were drafted, how would you feel?"

"That's a tough one, Mom. I'd put on the uniform and go proudly. Both my family and my girl would have to understand. I really want to do this but Dad will have to be involved also. Do you think he'll do it?"

"Yes, Jesse, I think he will."

Jesse casts his eyes to the floor and says, "There is one thing I haven't told you. Mr. O'Brien would like for Dad to come to the school board meeting Thursday night. Only if he approves and is willing to be involved with the flying club."

Joanne says, "That may be a problem. We'll talk to him after supper, okay?"

"Okay." Jesse walks over and kisses Joanne on the cheek. "Thanks, Mom. Now for my homework."

***

"Joanne, the supper was delicious," Mack tells her. "Now, what is the occasion? Don't act coy. You fixed all my favorite dishes. What do you have up your sleeve?"

Joanne answers, "Jesse and I read this brochure this afternoon, and after you read it, we would like to discuss it with you."

With a twinkle in his eye, Mack says, "Aha, the two of you are going to gang up on me, are you?"

Both of them hang their heads, and Jesse says, "Caught again. We can't get anything past him, can we?"

"No, we can't. We'll let you read, and after the dishes are done, we'll come into the study, and the three of us will decide what will or can be done. With a step, Joanne reaches down and kisses Mack on the forehead.

Jesse and Joanne walk into the study to find Mack staring into the fireplace. He looks up and says, "I like the idea. Tell me what I have to do. Where do we go from here?"

Jesse and Joanne both yell, "Hurrah!"

Chapter 29

Joanne is in the kitchen getting a cup of coffee. She glances at the clock and thinks, *They should be home anytime. I wonder how Jesse liked his first day. It doesn't seem possible that he is almost 18 and making such important decisions about his life. I'm so glad Mack married me and Jesse thinks of me as his mother. God has been good to me.*

The door opens, and Jesse comes bouncing into the kitchen. With a twinkle in his eye, he says, "Hi, Mom. You'll never guess what happened! I was so good, they are going to let me fly solo next week!"

Joanne looks from him to Mack and Mack shakes his head. She walks over and hugs Jesse. "I knew I had a smart son, I didn't realize just how smart."

Laughing and hugging her back, Jess remarks, "I told Dad I could fool you. We got our instructions today and our homework. It isn't going to be as easy as I thought. I still want to do it. We did get to go inside the plane, but Mr. O'Brien said it would be several weeks before we'd be able to fly."

Mack remarks, "I think it will be several months. However, the boys are so enthused about learning, I could be wrong."

"You are, Dad. I'm going to devote one hour a day to studying the manual and learning the contents of the book. It won't take as long as you think."

Joanne asks, "How many boys are in your class?"

Jesse groans, "Mom, really! It's not a class but a club. I think if it was a class, we wouldn't enjoy it half as much or want to do the homework. Anyway, there are 10 of us. The club is limited to 12."

"Mr. O'Brien has closed the membership as of today." Mack then picks up a cup and pours himself some coffee.

Jesse starts for the door, turns, and says, "I'm going to my room. I want to start my homework for next week."

Joanne and Mack exchange glances and say, “Good.”

“I’ve never seen him so enthused about anything before. I believe he will learn to fly.”

Joanne walks over to Mack and says, “Yes, and I think this will help him decide what career he wants to pursue.”

Kissing her, he says, “As usual, I think you’re right.”

***

As soon as he reaches his room, Jesse picks up the phone, dials a number, and flops down on the bed.

“Diane?” After a pause, he says, “I wanted you to be the first to know. I really enjoyed today, and I can’t wait to go up in the plane.

“Of course not, we’ll see each other, except I’ll have extra homework, not only my schoolwork but also for the club.

“Ah, Honey,” he says, “not when the club is preparing you for your future, and this one does.

“Diane, I’ll take you to the dance Friday, but you have to understand that my flying club will come first if there is a conflict in dates. This is my future, and I’m hoping you will be part of it, but that is your decision

“Maybe we should talk about the club face to face. You need to know that I won’t give up my dream of flying. This is my future, and I think I’d like to be a commercial pilot. They make a lot of money, and families fly free. You could go with me all over the world. Wouldn’t you like that?

“Good, I’ll see you at school tomorrow.

“Okay, ‘bye.”

Jesse hangs the phone up and lays there staring at the ceiling. Slowly he gets up, walks to his desk, and starts reading his club manual.

Chapter 30

Jesse rushes into the house yelling, "Mom, Mom!"

Joanne comes from the kitchen wiping her hands on her apron. "What's the matter?"

"Nothing's wrong, Mom," Jesse replies. "I want to tell you about the meeting."

"Okay, but let's sit down first. Would you like a cup of hot chocolate?"

"That sounds good."

Mack enters and says, "Does that include me?"

Walking over to him, Joanne kisses him and answers, "Of course it does."

Pouring the hot chocolate and then sitting down, Joanne says, "How about telling me about your meeting with the Blue Skye Flying Club?"

"The great thing is...I get to go up in the plane next week! Look out, sky, here I come!"

Mack shakes his head and says, "You'd think he is flying the plane, but he'll only be a passenger."

"Now, Mack, getting to go up in a plane that he'll eventually get to fly solo is a big deal." Joanne turns to Jesse and says, "I'm so proud of you. When you take your solo flight, I'll be there with the camera."

Mack raises his eyebrows and asks, "Will you take my picture, also? I'll be taking my solo flight at the same time."

Surprise comes over Joanne's face and she says, "I didn't realize you were learning to fly also. Of course I'll take your picture. It'll be fun to have two pilots in the family."

Mack winks at Jesse and taking a deep breath he stands and walks over to Joanne. He bends down, kisses her and says, "We could have three pilots if you'd be interested in flying."

"Let me think about that for awhile."

Jesse looks at them and makes a request, “Mom, we’re going to learn the survivor techniques, and I think it will be fun for all of us. Mr. O’Brien gave us permission to bring an interested person to the club meeting next week. Dad and I talked it over and decided we would like for you to go.”

“Wait a minute,” Joanne says with surprise in her voice. “What are you two planning to do? Throw me out of an airplane?”

Laughing, Mack tells her, “That’s exactly what we intend to do. Don’t panic; we’ll put a parachute on you first.”

“Sounds like fun,” Joanne says as she takes a piece of her hair and gives it a twist. “Then I’ll make my mind up about flying.”

“Good,” Jesse says, and he stands. “I’ve got homework so I’ll leave you ‘til later.”

Chapter 31

"It's been a long time since we got together," Joanne tells Tom and Mary. "Mary, I'm so glad you called me. Cherokee Park has always been my favorite spot."

Swallowing a bite of her sandwich, Mary says, "I'm glad too. We haven't gotten together since Jesse started high school. I don't even think we've talked on the phone."

Tom shakes his head and declares, "You quit taking my phone calls, and I've had to get a new model. There will never be one that the camera loves as much as it does you."

Joanne laughs, "You both are making me feel guilty, when in fact I've missed you just as much. Being a mother and a wife as well as the social butterfly doesn't leave much time for me or what I like to do.

"Jesse joined a flying club, and one of the requirements is for Mack to attend with him. They meet on Saturdays. As you can guess, we don't entertain on Saturdays or plan any weekend excursions."

Tom says, "Sounds very boring to me. So what do you do while they are playing 'Sky King'? You could model for me on Saturdays, couldn't you?"

Laughing, Joanne answers, "You never give up, do you? I read, answer letters or phone calls, and sometimes I bake cookies or make supper. I'm never bored, and they are so excited when they come home. I wouldn't think of doing anything that might take me from home longer than they would be gone. No, Tom, I won't try to squeeze a modeling job into that window. I wish you'd realize that I'm happier than I've ever been in my life."

"Believe me, Joanne," Mary says, "it shows. I've been thinking maybe Mike and I could find the kind of happiness that you and Mack have found without a lot of money. It might be fun to plan for each thing we want to do."

"Oh, Mary!" Joanne exclaims, "I know you could, and you'd be so happy. Of course, you wouldn't want a baby right away. Take some time to enjoy each other, at least for a couple of years. When do you want to start planning your wedding?"

Jumping to his feet, Tom throws down his sandwich and yells, "Hold on, this isn't what we agreed on back home when we were kids, or don't you remember? Joanne, you may have hit it rich, but you agreed to split the money with us. Looks to me like you got the best of the deal, and you're being very selfish by keeping it all to yourself."

Startled by his reaction, both girls look at each other. Mary is the first to speak, "Tom, grow up. I bet you have a tidy sum in the bank. Could it be you're greedy and want Joanne to do what you want? I think you're putting her friendship with us in jeopardy. I've decided, I'm going to tell Mike I want to set the date."

Tom sits back down, hanging his head and says, "I'm sorry, but I thought I had a way to see you, Joanne, every week. Will we be able to see Jesse take his solo flight?"

Hiding her feelings, Joanne answers, "Apology accepted, and yes, I'll invite both of you to his first solo flight. I can't wait for this Saturday! The club is going to teach the boys and their fathers how to survive a plane in trouble. They will be learning to sky dive, and I've been invited to go along. If I like it, and that's a big if, how would you both like to make a weekend a fun trip of sky diving?"

"I'm not sure," Mary tells her. "I've never been inside of a plane."

"Mary, they tell me it's a grand feeling." Joanne says as she reaches for Mary's hand. "I've never done either myself, but I'm willing to try."

"Count me in," Tom says. "I've got to leave; I have a photo shoot this afternoon. Sure wish it was you."

"Tom, forget about me," Joanne tells him. "I'll never model again and definitely not for you."

"That hurts, Joanne." Tom says as he hangs his head. "I thought someday you'd pose for me again, especially if something happened to Mack."

"No, Tom," she answers. "I would still have Jesse and all of the commitments of my civic duties. No, my modeling days are definitely over."

Mary stands and says, "I've got to go back to work. Let me know when you want me to sky dive with you." She walks away.

Tom turns to leave and says, “If you ever change your mind, let me know.”

“Don’t hold your breath,” Joanne says as she turns to look at the scenery.

Chapter 32

Walking from the airplane, Jesse turns to Joanne and says, "Gee, Mom, wasn't that fun? I know what I want to do when I graduate from high school."

Laughing, Joanne says, "Just what would that be?"

He answers, "I want to be a commercial pilot. I can't think of any job I'd like more. Think of it, up in the sky every day. It's so beautiful with all the blue around you, and the sun is so beautiful when it rises and sets. Mom, when I start to land, the scenery beneath me is so spectacular; the farm land looks like a patchwork quilt. Besides, Mom, I feel so close to God when I'm flying. I can't imagine doing anything except being a pilot." He gives a little laugh. "The girls at school think I'm something special because I'm learning to fly. Can you imagine what it would be like if I was a pilot? I'd have my pick of any girl I wanted."

Mack shakes his head and says, "That sounds like every boy's dream. However, I would hope your upbringing and your love of God would keep you from taking advantage of the girls who throw themselves at you."

"Dad, you don't have to worry, I'll never do anything to disgrace you and Mom."

"Jesse," Joanne says, "that's good to hear. Can we go eat? I'm hungry."

"Sure," Mack says as he starts toward the car.

"Wait a minute!" Mr. O'Brien calls as he runs toward them.

They stop and turn as he comes up to them.

"Jesse," Mr. O'Brien says, "with your parents' permission, how would you like a part time job?"

"If it was here," Jesse says, "I'd love it."

"Let's go to the Airport Café and have lunch. Then, I can tell you about the job, the hours, and, most importantly, the pay."

Mack says, "Sounds good to me, but are you sure the Airport

Café will let Jesse in? I always thought it was strictly for people over 21."

Mr. O'Brien answers, "Basically that's true. However, they have a small dining area in the back for the flyers and their families."

"I'm all for it," Joanne tells them. "Maybe Jesse will get to meet some of the other pilots, and he could find out the disadvantages too."

"It does sound like a winner," Mack says and turning to Mr. O'Brien. "We'll meet you there."

***

Sitting at the table, Jesse is the first one to speak, "I can't wait any longer, Mr. O'Brien. What is the job, and why do you think I can do it?"

Laughing, Mr. O'Brien says, "Aren't we curious?" Not waiting for an answer, he continues, "The job would be on an as needed basis, and you'd be learning at the same time. Some of the duties would be to check the equipment like parachutes and food supplies, loading and unloading luggage, and talking to the passengers. It would be after school and on Saturdays and Sundays. The pay starts at the minimum wage, and you'd start this week."

"Let me think about it. What a come down from learning to fly to gofer. What do you think, Dad?"

"Well, Son," Mack says, "you can't start at the top, and you need to know what is required on a plane to make the passengers comfortable and safe. Of course it's entirely up to you, but I think it would be a great experience, and you'd be learning whether you really want to be a pilot."

Joanne speaks up, "That's right, but Jesse it may put a damper on your love life. I know Diane isn't too happy with the time your club takes. The job would be another challenge to both of you."

Turning to Mr. O'Brien, Jesse asks, "How soon do you need my answer?"

"I'd like to know by Monday morning," Mr. O'Brien answers.

***

They drive in silence with each one lost in their own thoughts.

Finally, Mack breaks the silence, “I enjoyed the food, and Mr. O’Brien is very entertaining. Isn’t he, Jesse?”

“Yes, Dad, he is. I really liked the story of when he was flying for the Air Lift in Alaska. I may want to check further into the possibilities. I think they have the Air Lift planes in remote places like Wyoming, Oregon, and Utah to transport emergency patients to the hospitals.”

Laughing, Joanne says, “Would you be able to meet any girls or see the world?”

Laughing with her, Jesse answers, “If I was a pilot, the girls would seek me out regardless of where I worked. Anyway, I have college before I look at a permanent job. It’s just a thought.”

Mack states, “It’s a very noble one. Do you remember how long it takes for the training?”

“No, I don’t, but I bet Mom does, don’t you?”

“Sorry, Son,” Joanne says, “I don’t. I like the idea of you flying for Air Lift because back home they used them to fly some patients to Louisville for medical treatment. It saved a lot of lives.”

Thoughtfully, Jesse says, “I think I’ll bring up the subject next Saturday. Then we can all get the information at the same time.”

“That’s a very good idea,” Mack states.

“By the way,” Joanne says, “When I had lunch with Mary and Tom the other day, I suggested we get together and sky dive. Tom said he thought Jesse might want to explore the possibility of becoming an aerial photographer. He still thinks Jesse has a talent for taking photos. What do you think?”

Excited, Jesse exclaims, “I hadn’t thought of that, but I like the idea! I could get Diane to write an article for the school newspaper, and I could take the pictures of our excursion. Tom could help me with the best shots. I like the idea. Maybe Diane could come too.”

“Sounds good to me,” Mack states. “I’ve wanted to shove Tom out of a plane for the way he looks at your mother.”

Laughing, Joanne says, “You know that isn’t true. You’re the only one I love or will ever love.” She leans over and kisses him.

“Not while I’m driving, Hon. I have to watch the road.”

“Well?” Jesse asks.

“Of course,” Mack says. “I think it’s a good idea. You might as well experience all the possibilities of a flying career.”

Joanne asks, “When shall we go?”

“Jesse, how about next Sunday?” Mack asks.

“It would have to be on Sunday, because that is the only day we have free," Jesse answers.

"Let's make a day of it," Joanne suggests. "We'll all go to church together, eat lunch, take to the skies about two, and have a snack after we land."

"That a sounds good," Mack says.

Chapter 33

Sitting in Mary's living room, Mike and Tom are having their second cup of coffee. Tom asks, "Mike do you know how to sabotage a parachute?"

"No, I don't," Mike answers. "Why do you ask?"

"If you remember," Tom states, "I was going to push Mack off the cliff at Natural Bridge. Mary turned her ankle. We have been invited to go sky diving with them this Sunday, and I thought maybe I could sabotage his parachute."

"I think you're crazy! Can't you see Joanne loves him? Jesse is a great kid, and he looks up to you. I bet it was his idea to invite you since he wants to learn about taking photos from the air. How can you think of doing something that will hurt so many people?"

Tom stands up and starts pacing the floor. Turning to look at Mack, he says, "I can think of doing this because I'm in love with Joanne. If Mack is out of the way, she'll turn to me, like she always has. I'll make her love me. It WILL be worth it."

"Not if you get caught," Mike tells him.

"I won't get caught. Everyone will think it's an accident."

Shaking his head, Mike says, "You hope."

"That's okay," Tom tells him. "I don't want anyone to know what I'm planning or when it'll happen."

Walking into the room, Mary speaks, "My, you both look like the cat that ate the canary. What have you been up to?"

Rising Mike goes to her and says, "Nothing much. Tom was telling me about the plans to sky dive Sunday."

Kissing him, Mary says, "I don't know whether to be afraid and run for the hills or to close my eyes and let them push me from the plane."

"Aw, shucks, ma'am," Mike says while hanging his head and scuffing his foot, "they won't do anything to harm you. If they do, they'll have to answer to me."

Laughing, she takes his hand, looks into his eyes, "I wish you were going with us."

"Me, too, but you know what they say about three being a crowd."

***

Mr. O'Brien is reading a magazine while waiting for the group to show up to sky dive. Tom and Mary are the first to arrive.

"Good afternoon." Tom says as he extends his hand, "You must be Mr. O'Brien."

Taking Tom's hand, he says, "Yes, I am."

"I'm Tom Watson, and this is Mary Jones. We're with the Stevens."

"Yes, they told me you would be joining us today."

Tom scratches his head and says, "I'm looking forward to it, but I'm a little apprehensive about going. I've never done this before, and neither has Mary."

Mr. O'Brien gives a small laugh and tells him, "Don't worry, we go over the parachutes with a fine tooth comb before they are put on the plane. Before you jump they're inspected again. So you can see, Tom, it's perfectly safe. The only thing that could go wrong ... would be you'd forget to pull the ripcord. Then you could break your neck when you landed."

With tongue in cheek, Tom says, "Did I forget to tell you that I have a memory problem?"

Laughing, Mary takes Tom's arm and says, "You'd better be good, or I'll throw you out without the parachute. Maybe I'll cut the ripcord."

Just then Joanne, Mack, Jesse, and Diane walk in. Introductions are made, and Mack says, "Let's get this show on the road." He then walks over to the parachutes and starts handing them out.

"Let's check our equipment before putting it on." Mr. O'Brien tells them.

They each pick up a parachute and look at each other. Standing in front of the group, Mr. O'Brien gives them instructions. "Look for small holes or tears on the outside of the pack. If you see one, call me, and I'll check it out. Next look at the ripcord. It should be long enough that you won't have to search for it and should be in the middle and front of the pack. If it isn't, call me, and I'll check it out." He gives them a few minutes to complete the examination and says, "Okay, let's put them on. Remember the pack is on your back. The rip cord should be close to your left shoulder and within easy reach. I'll inspect each one again before we jump. Let's go."

Ah ha! Tom thinks. *I'll get close enough to cut the ripcord in the back. No one will notice, and he won't be able to get the chute open. I couldn't have picked a better time.*

Tom walks over and puts his hand on Mack's shoulder. "Mack, oh boy, I'm so glad you invited Mary and me to do this with you. I'm excited, and I think I'll even take some flying lessons. Maybe, you'd be willing to help me? I can think of a lot of things flying could help me with in my profession."

"Sure, Tom," Mack answers. "If you wouldn't mind I'll bring Jesse along, and you could give him tips on taking photos from the air."

"Jesse has already mentioned it to me." With a swift movement of his hand, Tom cuts the ripcord.

"You do know, Tom, I'll be with you and Jesse every time you fly."

"Yes, Mack, and you'll always be welcome."

***

Mr. O'Brien opens the door and announces, "Don't forget to count to 1000 before pulling the ripcord. You wait until you see the parachute open on the descending jumper before you jump. Okay?"

"Okay," they all murmur.

***

Mack jumps first. He reaches for the ripcord and pulls, nothing happens, He pulls it again, and the cord comes off his shoulder and drops over his hand. He panics and starts kicking his legs and flailing his arms trying to fly like a bird. He prays, *Please God help me. Let me fall and not be seriously hurt. If it is Your will to take me home, please take care of Joanne and Jesse. Please God help me. Not my will, but Thine be done. Amen.*

***

Joanne watches and counts. She panics and turning to Mr.

O'Brien she screams, "His chute isn't opening! Do something! Hurry! Help him!"

Without answering, Mr. O'Brien shoves everyone out of the way and jumps. He prays, *Please God help me reach him in time, and may we both land with very few injuries. I ask this in Jesus' name. Not my will, but Thine be done.*

If he keeps kicking and flailing his arms I may be able to reach him. God willing I can hold on to him when the parachute stops me for a second before letting us descend. I'm almost to the point to pull my cord. Here goes nothing.

Mr. O'Brien reaches for Mack. Mack realizing that someone is reaching for him, throws himself toward his rescuer and grabs Mr. O'Brien around the waist as Mr. O'Brien grabs Mack's arms.

Mr. O'Brien gives a sigh of relief as Mack holds on for dear life, and he thinks *Thank You, God, for helping me to reach Mack in time.*

Everyone clusters around the door watching with their hearts in their mouths. Joanne is watching and twisting her hair.

No one speaks, but silently each is counting to 1000. Mr. O'Brien doesn't open his chute. Joanne screams, "What is he thinking? Will both of them be killed? God, please help them!"

Jesse walks over and takes his mother in his arms. He has tears running down his cheeks. "Mom, please have faith. Whatever is God's will we'll have to accept. It may not be easy, but He'll give us the strength we need. Please trust Him. I do."

Joanne slumps into his arms and sobs.

Mary just stands in pure shock. Then the chute opens and Mary screams, "The chute opened, and Mack is still holding on. They're descending. Thank God they're safe."

Walking to the door both Jesse and Joanne look and give a sigh of relief.

Tom shakes his head and says, "I wonder why the cord didn't work. Mr. O'Brien checked everyone's chute before we put them on and again after we got into the plane. Did he overlook something?"

"I don't think so." Jesse answers, "Sometimes fluke accidents happen. They're not anyone's fault. It's God's way of showing us life is very fragile, and He can take us home in a moment's notice."

Mary says, "Look, they're on the ground. I think they're safe."

The pilot says, "Now that that is over, does anyone else want to jump?"

Jesse says, "Yes, I do. I want to make sure they both got safely to the ground with no injuries."

Joanne just states, "I'm going now," and she jumps.

Jesse counts to 1000, watches her chute open and then he jumps. Tom and Mary follow suit.

Landing within a few feet of Mack and Mr. O'Brien, Jesse and Joanne take the harnesses off and rush to them.

"Are you hurt?" Joanne asks.

Mack answers, "I have a bruised ego, and my leg hurts. I can't move it. Joanne, will you move it for me?"

"No, Honey, I won't. The ambulance is on its way, and the attendant will do what is necessary to make you comfortable. I'll go to the hospital with you if Mr. O'Brien will take Jesse home. I'm sure Tom and Mary are too shaken up to be of much help."

Tom stands to one side and says, "Looks like you have everything under control. I'll take Mary home. If you need anything, please call me."

"Okay." Mack and Joanne answer.

Jesse protests, "I want to be with Dad."

"It's okay, Jess." Mr. O'Brien tells him. "I need to see what is wrong with your dad's leg, so you can go with me to the hospital, and if you need a place to stay, I have a guest room."

"Thanks a million," Mack tells him.

***

Entering the waiting room, the doctor walks over to Joanne and asks, "Mrs. Stevens?"

Rising, she answers, "Yes, Doctor?"

"Mrs. Stevens, your husband is being taken to a room. His leg was broken, but we want to keep him overnight for observation. As soon as he's settled, you may see him."

"Thank you, Doctor."

The doctor leaves the room, and Joanne turns to Mr. O'Brien and says, "If your offer to keep Jesse tonight still stands, I'd like to stay with Mack."

He answers, "I'd be very pleased to keep Jesse out of trouble tonight. We'll leave after he sees his dad."

Jesse looks from one to the other and says, "Did either of you think I might want to spend the night here? Close to my dad? No, you both think I'm still in diapers and anything you say I'll have to like. Well I DON'T."

Joanne rushes to his side puts an arm around his shoulder and says, "You're right. We didn't think, but tomorrow is a school day. Id I remember correctly, you have a test in history. Isn't that so?"

"Y ... y ... yes, but I feel like Dad needs me more." He answers as he hangs his head.

"Okay," Joanne tells him, "we'll make a decision after we see your dad."

Mr. O'Brien walks over, touches Jesse's arm, and remarks, "The offer still stands if you want it."

"Okay," Jesse answers.

Chapter 34

As soon as Mr. O'Brien and Jesse leave, Joanne leans over and kisses her husband.

Mack kisses her and says, "I love you. Have you noticed that Tom and Mary aren't here? If they were true friends they wouldn't have left your side. Do you think they were hoping I'd die?"

"Don't be ridiculous, Mack. They feel very deeply for both of us, and everyone handles emergencies differently. I'll probably have a dozen phone calls from them when I get home. It wouldn't surprise me if they show up here in a few moments with food for us both."

"You may be right, but I can't help feeling that they want me out of the way."

"Oh, Honey, you've had a close call. I understand you want to blame somebody, but surely you can't think they had anything to do with the parachute failing to open. Can you?"

"I've told you before; I see the way Tom looks at you. I've never seen him look at Mary that way, nor have I seen him hold her hand. What am I to think?"

"Absolutely nothing. I love you, and I haven't modeled for a long time. I haven't any desire to return to that life. My world revolves around you and Jesse. I've never been happier. You have nothing to worry about, but I think you had better rest. I'll stay here beside you."

"Thanks, Love," and he turns over on his side.

***

Mr. O'Brien has sat quietly beside Jesse while driving home. When he turns into the drive he asks, "Do you think you can sleep now?"

"I'm not sure," Jesse answers. "I know Dad is going to make it, but I can't help wondering if this was an accident."

"Son, I wouldn't let that worry me. We'll have the report from the inspector in a few days, and then we'll know for sure."

"I know," Jesse says, "but I keep going over in my mind what happened, and I'm sure it wasn't an accident. When Tom put his hand on Dad's shoulder, he let it slip for a second to Dad's back. Could he have cut the ripcord?"

"I'm not sure." Mr. O'Brien reaches for the door handle and starts to get out. "Come on, Jesse, we'll have a cup of coffee for me and hot chocolate for you and then to bed."

Getting out of the car, Jesse says, "Sounds good to me."

***

As soon as they get into the car and start for Mary's apartment, Mary turns to Tom and says angrily, "I thought you'd given up on the idea of killing Mack. It's been three years since the last time, and Joanne is so happy. Can't you see that?"

"Yes, but she'd be much happier with me especially with all that money. We'd do the same things she is doing now, and I do like Jesse. He's a good kid. I could teach him about photography. He'll make a great photographer someday ... with my guidance."

"Boy, are you conceited! All you think about is yourself. I don't know you anymore, and I don't think I want to."

"Mary, I'm the same person. All I want is what Joanne, you, and I talked about when we were kids. The only one who's hit the jackpot is Joanne, and she promised to share. Don't you want to get married? I know Mike does."

"Yes, I do, but not at the expense of making Joanne unhappy. In fact, I think I'll tell Mike I'm going to set the wedding date."

In shock, Tom turns to look at Mary and narrowly misses an oncoming car. He says, "Now look what you've done. You are as exasperating as Joanne. She's a great model. We could be a great team, but, no, she married Mack and now won't live up to her end of the bargain. And you are talking nonsense about getting married. Where does that leave me?"

"Working hard and saving every penny you can towards your goal of having money."

"Here we are. I don't want to hear another word about this!" Tom shouts as Mary gets out of the car.

Turning, she says, "I don't want to think you're trying to kill Mack ever again. If I do I'll go to the police." She doesn't wait for an answer but slams the car door and walks into the apartment building.

Chapter 35

Turning over and looking at Joanne, Mack asks, "How did you sleep, love?"

Laughing as she leans over and kisses him on the forehead, she answers, "Fine. You snored all night so I know how you slept. Breakfast will be served in a few minutes. Would you like a warm washcloth to wash your face and hands?"

"Yes, I would," he answers.

Joanne takes the washcloth to the bathroom and returns with it, some water, and soap. She then washes Mack's face and hands.

Looking adoringly at his wife, Mack takes Joanne's hand in his and says, "How did I ever get so lucky as to deserve you?"

Joanne kisses him on the forehead and answers, "I've always felt that God blessed me by putting you in my life. I've never been happier. I enjoy being with you and Jesse on our little outings ... even when they put you in the hospital."

Becoming quite serious Mack says, "Joanne, do you really think this was an accident?"

"I'm not sure," she answers, "but I sure hope so. I don't know of anyone wanting to hurt you."

Taking her hand again, he says, "Think about it. The parachutes were new, and they were inspected before we put them on. Nothing was found wrong, so why did it fail to open?"

"I'm sure it was just a tear so small nobody could see it."

"I hope so. I'd hate to think someone did this deliberately."

"So would I." Joanne takes the water and washcloth back to the bathroom.

The nurse comes in with the breakfast tray and asks, "How are you feeling this morning, Mr. Stevens?"

"I feel good, and I hope the doctor sends me home today," Mack answers.

The nurse then turns to Joanne and asks, "Would you like

some breakfast?"

"Yes, I would. Thank you."

Joanne rolls the bed up to a near sitting position and arranges the breakfast tray.

Mack starts to eat and says, "Am I going to get this same kind of treatment at home? If not I'll stay right here."

Joanne reaches for the tray and tells him, "I was thinking about it, but since you put it that way I'll take your breakfast away until you say uncle."

Laughing, Mack pulls the tray back towards him, winks at Joanne, and says, "Love, I don't care how you treat me. I just want to go home."

The nurse comes in with a breakfast tray for Joanne. She sets it on the bedside table and asks, "Is there anything else?"

Mack and Joanne both answer together, "No thank you." They burst out laughing.

The nurse laughs and says, "Two great minds run together." She turns and walks out of the room.

"I wonder how long it will be before the doctor comes in," Mack says.

Joanne says, "I understand he always comes in during the morning. If that's the case he should be here shortly. How is your breakfast? Mine is very good."

"No one can beat your cooking, but since I'm a prisoner, I have to say it was pretty good."

Joanne laughs and says, "Compliments won't get you home any quicker. You'll still have to go by what the doctor says."

"You're right, but I'm allowed to be impatient, aren't I?"

Joanne leans over and kisses Mack on the forehead. Straightening, she says, "Yes, Dear, you are, but remember when I get you home I'll make you behave, and you won't have a soul to defend you."

Mack makes himself shake and says, "See what you've done! I'm shaking in my boots."

"Sorry, Darling ,but you don't have boots on." Joanne then sits down on the chair and picks up a magazine.

Chapter 36

"It's good to be home," Mack says.

Joanne sits down and sighs, "Yes it is. However, I think I'm going to have to have help with you. The wheel chair is hard to push, and I'm out of shape."

Reaching for her hand Mack tells her, "Honey, if you need help get it. I'll learn to navigate this chair and to make myself useful. Give me a feather duster, and watch me go."

Joanne laughs, rises, and kisses Mack. She asks, "Would you like a cup of coffee?"

Mack answers, "Yes I would, and to show you how efficient I am. I'll wheel myself to the kitchen."

"Please don't overdo. The doctor told you to take it easy, and in a week or two you can try crutches."

Mack makes a face at her and says, "I'll call Mary and have her bring over my work. I think I can work from the den and stay out of your hair."

With tongue in cheek Joanne replies, "My hair isn't long enough for you to get into it." She turns to walk away.

Mack reaches for her, but she is out of reach. He then starts wheeling towards the kitchen.

***

The doorbell rings, and Joanne goes to answer it. Standing there is Mr. O'Brien holding a file. Joanne says, "Come in, Mr. O'Brien. Mack is in the den. I'll get you both a cup of coffee."

He says, "Good, but I'll wait until you come back because I need to talk to both of you."

"Okay, then I'll hurry." Joanne starts toward the kitchen then turns back to Mr. O'Brien says, "I'm sorry, I forgot: This is the first time you've been here. The den is to your left. Go on in; Mack will be glad to see you."

Mr. O'Brien starts for the den and calls over his shoulder, "Hurry with the coffee, I'm dying for a cup."

Entering the den, Mr. O'Brien extends his hand to Mack and then sits down. He says, "I got the report back on the parachute. I want to wait for Joanne because this involves both of you, if that's okay with you."

"By all means we'll wait for Joanne. I had Mary bring my work from the bank, and I'm able to work here in the den without interruptions." Laughing, Mack adds, "I may transfer my complete office here."

"I doubt that Joanne would like that, and definitely the bank wouldn't," Mr. O'Brien answers.

Joanne enters with a tray of coffee and cookies. Mr. O'Brien stands and offers to take the tray. Joanne shakes her head and sets the tray on the table. She then hands the coffee to Mr. O'Brien and Mack and takes a cup for herself.

Sitting down, she says, "Help yourself to the cookies. What is in the report?"

Taking a bite of cookie, Mr. O'Brien says, "The chute didn't open because the cord had been cut just enough that when you pulled the cord it tore. It's a shame you panicked and didn't pull the emergency cord. This was a miracle of the highest degree. There is only a second of a window for me to grab Mack, and I had to have a strong enough hold not to drop him. When the parachute opens, it stops all movement of the jumper. The jumper is traveling at 120 miles per hour, then the parachute pulls you up before you start your descent. It was a miracle that you grabbed me. We're very lucky that all you got was a broken leg, aren't we?"

"Yes we are," Joanne and Mack say gratefully.

"I brought the complete report for you to read and keep. The investigators will be coming to question you about the jump and to see if you had a reason to attempt suicide. I thought I could help by going over the afternoon with you before they get here."

Mack folds his hands in front of him and says, "I'm glad you did, but I can't think of anyone or anything that might have cut the cord. Can you, Joanne?"

Mack watches Joanne very closely as she ponders the question. She looks at Mack wondering what he is thinking and says, "I can't think of a soul. Surely you don't suspect one of us in the plane, do you?"

Mr. O'Brien looks at his coffee, raises his head and says, "If someone in the plane didn't cut the cord then I overlooked the obvious when we inspected the parachutes before putting them on. I have gone over the inspection in my mind, and I can't remember seeing a cut then or after we boarded the plane. Can you remember anything out of the ordinary?"

Joanne lowers her eyes and replies, "This may or may not be important, but I saw Tom put his arm around Mack's shoulder, and then he slid his hand down his back."

Mack says in a huff, "I think Tom loves Joanne, and I think he wishes I'd die so he could have her."

"Don't be silly, Mack," Joanne says. "He knows I love you and would never do anything to harm you or our marriage."

"So, you do know he's in love with you," Mack says.

"Hold on a minute!" Mr. O'Brien exclaims. "I didn't want to start a family argument, but it seems to me that Tom should be questioned about the afternoon. Wouldn't you agree?"

"Yes," Joanne says, "and the sooner the better."

"I agree." Mack says nodding his head .

"Then it's settled," Mr. O'Brien says as he rises from the chair. "I'll tell the investigators to come see you and to continue the investigation. I don't know what the outcome will be, but I wish you luck."

Joanne walks Mr. O'Brien to the door and says, "Thanks for stopping by, and please do come again."

He says, "I will, and thanks for the coffee," and he walks out the door.

Joanne walks back to the den, stands at the door a minute, and says, "Do you think Tom could have cut the cord?"

"Yes, I do," Mack answers. "I know he loves you, and I think he would have backed me over that cliff the first time we went camping, but I was saved by Mary turning her ankle."

"You may be right. What are we going to tell the inspectors? What if we're wrong, and he didn't have a thing to do with it?" Turning to look at Mack, Joanne wrings her hands and sighs. She walks to a chair and sits down.

Mack reaches for her hand and says, "Honey, I know how close you are to Mary and Tom, but we have to face facts. He is in love with you, and I think he'd do anything to get you back in his life, both as a model and as his wife. I didn't tell you, but a couple of weeks ago someone cut the guide wire in the steering column on my car while I was at work. The garage attendant told me a mechanic had taken my car to check out a problem. I stopped at a garage on my way home, and the mechanic found and fixed the problem. I didn't want you to worry so I didn't tell you. We need to tell the inspector everything including any and all suspicions."

"Yes, we should, and let the chips fall where they may." Joanne answers as nods fervently.

Chapter 37

Joanne is drying the dishes when the door bell rings. She goes to the door and there stands a gentleman she doesn't know. She asks, "May I help you?"

"Yes, you may," Mr. Nixon answers. "I'm Mr. Nixon, the inspector for the Federal Aviation Board, and I want to interview you and your husband. May I come in?"

Joanne steps from in front of the door and says, "By all means do come in. Mack is in the den. That is the room to your left. If you'll go on in and introduce yourself, I'll get us all a cup of coffee."

"Thank you," Mr. Nixon says as he starts for the den.

Joanne enters with the coffee and some cookies. She hands a cup to each of the men, takes her cup, and sits down.

Mr. Nixon takes a sip of coffee and says, "As you know I'm here to ask questions about your accident. We do treat it as an accident until we're convinced otherwise. Mack, I'd like to hear your version first."

Clearing his throat, Mack says, "It was a beautiful day. We were going to jump for the second time with a couple of friends and our son's girlfriend. It was the first time for our guests. The parachutes were inspected by Mr. O'Brien before we put them on. After we put them on he inspected them again to make sure we had tightened the belts and had them situated correctly. He gave us the okay, and we sat down. Everyone followed suit except for Tom. He was one of the guests. He walked over to me and put his hand on my shoulder. I'm sorry, but I don't remember what he said. As he started to walk away he let his hand slide down my back. I feel that if anyone could have cut the cord it would be him."

Looking puzzled, Mr. Nixon asks, "Why would you suspect a friend of doing this?"

Taking in a deep breath Mack looks at Joanne, lowers his head and answers, "Because he is in love with my wife. He thinks if I'm out of the way he'll have a chance to marry her. I don't believe my wife feels the same way about him. There were a couple of other instances before this. When we first married, we went on a hiking trip. Tom is a photographer for an advertising company. Joanne was his top model. Anyway, Tom wanted a picture of me with the scenery in the background. He kept backing me up towards the edge of the cliff. If Mary, his supposed girlfriend, hadn't sprung her ankle I'd been lying at the bottom of the crevice. Then the guide wire on my car's steering column was cut while I was at work. Now this. No, Mr. Nixon, I don't think the cut on the parachute cord was an accident. I think Tom did it."

Before Mr. Nixon can answer, Joanne says, "I believe Mack is right. Tom, Mary, and I grew up together. We'd meet once a day for lunch. I should say to eat whatever we could find in the house to eat. We'd go to the creek and share what we found and talk about our futures. We made a vow that we'd leave the country and move to the city. We'd become millionaires by hook or by crook and share our fortunes with each other. I met Mack, fell in love, and married him. Tom resented the fact that I was the first to, by his outlook, obtain our goal. I thought our plan was a little silly after I grew up, and so did Mary. Tom wanted us to honor our commitment. We've tried to talk him out of holding us to this childhood dream. I thought we had. I hate to think Tom would do anything to hurt me or Mack, but I can't overlook the fact that Mack could have been killed. Believe me, I love my husband, and I've never been happier in my life. If anything happens to Mack I'd never think of marrying Tom. I'm sure I wouldn't ever want to see or hear from him again."

"Well you've certainly given me pause for thought," Mr. Nixon tells them. "Let's see if I have this straight. You, Mrs. Stevens, grew up with Tom Watson and Mary Jones. The three of you made a pact to become millionaires and to share the riches with each other. You were the first to hit the jackpot, and Tom resented it. He is and always has been in love with you, right?"

"Yes," Joanne answers.

Rising, Mr. Nixon says, "I think I have everything I need from you except for Tom's and Mary's addresses."

Joanne hands him a piece of paper. "Here is the information I thought you might need."

"Thank you. I'll let you know what I find out." Joanne walks Mr. Nixon to the door.

***

The doorbell rings, and Mike answers the door. Mr. Nixon extends his hand and says, "Hello, Mr. Watson. I'm Mr. Nixon. I need to ask some questions about the sky dive you attended with Mack Stevens."

"Come in, Mr. Nixon," Mike answers. "I'm Tom's brother. He should be home shortly. Would you like a cup of coffee?"

"Yes, I would," he answers as he sits down in the closest chair.

Mike gets coffee for both himself and Mr. Nixon. He hands the cup to Mr. Nixon and sits opposite him in the other chair. He says, "If you would like to ask some of the questions of me, I'll try to answer as truthfully as possible."

"I appreciate that." Mr. Nixon takes a sip of coffee and continues, "Mr. Stevens seems to think your brother is in love with his wife. What do you think?"

"They grew up together so naturally there is a closeness that only a lifetime of experiences together can bring." Mike glances away from Mr. Nixon and takes a sip of his coffee.

"Well, Mrs. Stevens told me about a childhood vow of becoming millionaires and of her effort to talk Mr. Watson out of wanting her to honor it. What do you think?"

Mike is so perplexed by Joanne being so honest that he takes a few minutes to answer. "I do know of the vow. I've wanted to marry Mary Jones for quite some time, but because of this silly vow she won't set the date. However, I don't think Tom had anything to do with the parachute not opening."

"I see," Mr. Nixon replies as glances through his notes. "What about the trip your brother and Mary Jones took with the Stevens to Natural Bridge Park? Do you think Mr. Stevens would have fallen over the cliff if Miss Jones hadn't sprained her ankle?"

"Since I wasn't there, I couldn't say. I do know Mack was posing for a photo shot with the scenery in the background, and he was standing on the rim of a crevice. Oh yes, Tom was taking the picture."

Rising to go Mr. Nixon says, "You've answered all the questions I had. I don't think I need to talk to your brother at this time. Oh, I forgot: A few days ago the guide wire in the steering column of Mr. Stevens' car was cut. Would you know anything about that?"

"No, I wouldn't," Mike says as he rises from his chair.

Walking to the door Mr. Nixon turns, extends his hand, and says, “Thank you for the coffee and the information. Tell your brother I was here, and if I need to talk to him I’ll call first.”

“Okay,” Mike says as he takes Mr. Nixon’s hand. “Tom will be sorry to have missed you.”

***

Answering the door, Mary says, “Hello, may I help you?”

“Yes,” Mr. Nixon answers, “I’m Mr. Nixon, and I hope you’re Mary Jones.”

“I’m Mary Jones, but what do you want with me?”

“I’m with the Federal Aviation Board, and I need to ask you some questions about the accident with Mack Stevens’ parachute not opening. May I come in?”

Stepping aside, Mary opens the door wider and says, “Do come in. May I get you some coffee?”

“No thanks, Miss Jones. This’ll only take a minute.” Mr. Nixon sits down. “Now let’s see. According to my notes this was the first time you were going to jump?”

“Yes, and we were all excited. Tom was teaching Jesse about aerial photographs before the jump, and Mack volunteered to jump first so Jesse could photograph him.”

“Do you mean to tell me that Jesse Stevens has photographs of the outing?”

“Yes. Didn’t anyone mention them before?”

“No, they didn’t. I have one more question, and then I’ll leave. Do you think Tom Watson could have cut the ripcord when he slid his hand down Mr. Stevens’ back?”

Mary hesitates, thinking for a few minutes, and says, “Maybe, but I don’t think Tom would do such a thing. I know when we were kids Joanne, Tom, and I made a vow to become rich, but we’ve all outgrown such a notion with age and maturity.”

, Mr. Nixon extends his hand and says, “Thanks for the information. If I need to ask more questions, I’ll call first.”

Mary walks him to the door and says, “Glad to be of help. Goodbye.”

Chapter 38

Driving home from Mary and Mike's wedding, Mack says, "That was a very simple and beautiful wedding. Wasn't it Joanne?"

"Yes, it was," Joanne answers. "I'm so happy for Mary. I know she and Mike will be as happy as we are. Turning to look at Jesse, she asks, "When will we get to see the photos you took?"

Jesse looks at Joanne and answers, "I'm going straight to my dark room when we get home. I should have them by tomorrow. I think I got some great shots."

"I'm sure you did, Jesse," Mack says. "By the way I was wondering why Tom didn't come, and why he didn't take the pictures. Anyone have a clue? Even Mr. O'Brien was asking about it."

Looking uncomfortable Joanne answers, "Mike asked that Tom not be in the wedding, and he also asked Jesse to do the photos as he felt that Tom is a threat to you and me."

Protesting, Mack remarks, "Tom is his brother, and if I'd had a brother when we married I'd have wanted him to be my best man. No one would have talked me out of it. So give. What's going on? What are you holding back?"

Jesse puts a hand on Mack's shoulder and says, "Dad, they couldn't prove that Tom cut the cord on your parachute, but they still suspect that he's tried to kill you. Mike decided that it was too risky for him to be at the wedding or to take the photos. Mike didn't want Tom to do something stupid that would make him go to jail."

Joanne tells them. "I've told Tom in front of Mary and Mike that I never want to see him again, and I definitely do not want to hear from him. Now you know why he wasn't at the wedding and Jesse was asked to take the photos. At least Jesse had Tom's influence with his photos. I know the wedding pictures will be great."

Mack asks, “All of this makes a lot of sense, but don’t you both think I’m capable of taking care of myself?”

They both look at each other and start laughing. “No,” Jesse says, “because if you were we wouldn’t have had to nurse you back to health after you hurled yourself from a plane.”

“Touché,” Mack says, “you’ve made your point.

They drive the rest of the way home in silence.

***

As soon as they enter the house, Joanne asks, “Mack, how about a cup of coffee and a cup of hot chocolate for you, Jesse?”

Mack answers, “I’d love a cup. Besides I have something to discuss with both of you.”

“Gee, Dad,” Jesse says, “I would like to beg off. I want to start on the photos as soon as possible. Okay?”

“Jesse, my lad,” Mack says as he puts an arm around Jesse’s waist, “I think when you hear what I have on my mind you’ll forget all about those pictures for tonight.”

“I guess it’s hot chocolate for me, Mom,” Jesse says as he heads for the kitchen.

Mack follows him to the kitchen, and when he passes Joanne he winks at her.

Joanne scratches her head and walks behind them. She goes straight to the cabinet and gets the cups and saucers out. Then she puts the coffee on and starts the hot chocolate. She sits down until the liquids are ready to pour. “Okay, give, Mack,” she says. “What is so important that Jesse couldn’t start working on his photos?”

With a twinkle in his eye and a sheepish grin, Mack gives a small laugh and says, “Maybe, just maybe, I wanted you both to sit in the kitchen with me for awhile.”

“Mack I know you better than that,” Joanne tells him as she rises to get the coffee and the hot chocolate. “How about telling us what you have on your mind?”

“Yeah, Dad, I’d like to know also.”

“Okay, okay. I’ll tell just as soon as we get our drinks and your mother sits down.”

Joanne sets a plate of cookies on the table. She then sets a cup of coffee in front of Mack and the hot chocolate in front of Jesse. She sits down with her cup. She reaches for a cookie and says, “Okay, Mack, we’re all ears. What did you want to talk about?"

"You know I go out of town for various bank functions, and I'm usually gone from one day to a week."

"Yes," Joanne says, "and we both know how you hate to be away from us."

"Well, in a few weeks both Jesse and I will have our pilot's license, and I was thinking maybe if the budget could stand it we might buy our own plane. Then you could go with me and Jesse could also if the trips were on the weekend or in the summer."

Jesse jumps up, runs to his dad, throws his arms around him and says, "I like the idea. I could experiment with my aerial photos and maybe get more experience with my flying. What do you say, Mom? Yes, I hope."

"This is so sudden!" Joanne exclaims as she puts her hand over her heart, "Could I have a month or a year to think about it?"

Mack laughs and says, "No, you can't. All I want to hear you say is, 'Honey, I think that's a great idea, and we'll do everything we can to let you have a new toy'."

Joanne ducks her head and says, "I'm teasing. I like the idea of being able to go with you. I could shop while you attend your meetings, and then we'd have the evenings together."

Mack heaves a sigh of relief and says, "That was easier than I thought it was going to be. I'll contact the airport tomorrow and have them to start looking for a plane. Yes, Jesse, you may be excused to develop your pictures."

"Good," Jesse says as he rises and leaves the room.

Chapter 39

The phone is ringing when Joanne enters the house. She rushes to answer it and just as she reaches the phone it quits ringing. *I wonder who that was. Well they'll call back, and then I'll know. It might have been Mary. She is due back today or tomorrow from her honeymoon, and I know she'll want to see the pictures of the wedding. I think they turned out great. Of course, I'm prejudiced because Jesse took them.*

The phone rings again, breaking into her thoughts. She answers, "Hello.

"No, he isn't. May I take a message?

"I'll let him know as soon as he comes home. How long will you be there?

"Yes, Mr. Zimmerman, he should be able to call you before you leave. Thank you for calling." She hangs the phone up and walks to the kitchen.

Jesse is excited as he walks into the kitchen, "Hi, Mom. Have you heard from Mary and Mike? They're due home today aren't they?"

Laughing, Joanne says, "No, I haven't heard from them, and yes, they are due home. I know how anxious you are to show your photos to them, but you'll just have to be patient."

Frowning, Jesse says, "It's important to me to know if my work is good enough for me to think about photography as a career. I can't wait to hear what they think."

Walking over to him Joanne puts her arm around him and gently says, "I think you're good enough and smart enough to do anything you put your mind to. Would you like a cup of hot chocolate?"

"No, Mom," he answers, "I need to work on my homework so I'll go upstairs and get busy. If you hear from them please let me know when they'll be over."

“I will,” Joanne says.

As Jesse starts out of the room, the phone rings. He stops as Joanne answers and waits to see who it is.

Turning to Jesse, Joanne says, “He’s standing here biting his fingernails to the quick. Would you like to talk to him?”

Joanne hands the phone to him and walks over to the sink.

“Hello,” he says.

“Yes, that will be fine. I’ll be here. Sure. Here’s Mom.” He signals for Joanne to take the phone.

Joanne takes the phone and says, “I’m back.

“Okay, we’ll see you about 8:00.” She hangs the phone up, turns to Jesse, and says, “I guess you can concentrate on your lessons now. Mary and Mike will be here at 8:00 tonight, and they are anxious to see the photos.”

“I sure can.” Jesse runs from the room and up the stairs.

Chapter 40

Looking up from the photos, Mary says, “Jesse, these are beautiful. You certainly know how to play the light and the positions of the people. I need to know when you decided to include various photos of the reception. The little girl peeking from behind her mother is darling. Did you get their names and permission to take the photo?”

Blushing, Jesse replies, “I took some pictures without the people’s knowledge, but afterward I told them that I had taken a picture and asked for their names and to sign a consent form for me. I told them I would send them a copy of the photo. Everyone signed the form and gave me their addresses.”

“I’m so proud of you, Jesse,” Mary says, “Have you looked closely at the pictures, Mike?”

“Yes, I have,” Mike answers. “My favorite is the one of you stooping down to talk to the little girl. She is so cute with her thumb in her mouth, and you were so intent on what you were saying to her. What is her name?”

Joanne says, “Her name is Florence. My favorite photo is of Mack and me dancing. Jesse did a great job of catching people at their best and being themselves.”

Mack stands and says, “Mike, I’d like to talk to you alone for a minute. Would you like to join me in the den?”

“Sure, Mack,” Mike says as he stands and follows him into the den.

Sitting down in a chair across from Mack, Mike asks, “What is this all about?”

“Mike I’m thinking of buying an airplane. It makes a lot of sense to me, but I need someone else’s opinion to help me decide.”

“Hold on a minute, Mack. I don’t know anything about planes, so I’m not sure I can help you decide.”

“Let me put it another way. I need a sounding board, and

you're it."

"In that case," Mike says while crossing his legs and settling in, "you have my full attention."

"Good. As you know, Mike, I have to attend meetings out of town. Commercial flights take time, and there are delays at the airports while waiting for a connecting flight. I love flying and everything connected with it. Jesse is still deciding on a career. You've seen what he can do with the camera, and if we had a plane it would open up another area for his photography. Also, Jesse can fly a plane as well if not better than I can. I could take Joanne with me on the business trips, and she could shop or explore the towns while I'm in meetings. Those are the good reasons to buy a plane. Now for the reasons not to: The plane would have to be stored at the airport for a fee plus a fee to a mechanic to maintain it. Not to mention the price of the plane. It would sit there for several months without being used and eat up money. Would the convenience of having a plane at my beck and call outweigh the expense of having my own plane?"

"Well," Mike says, "I know I said I couldn't give an opinion, but I'm going to. I don't think the plane would be sitting for months without moving. Since you and Jesse both love to fly, the plane would be like a second car. Joanne likes being with you, and I bet she'd never get tired of going to the various towns where you have your bank meetings. Jesse would learn how to take aerial photos. Who knows? He may become as famous as Ansel Adams. I think you've already sold yourself on the idea and just want someone to tell you it's a good idea. I think it is."

"Thank you, Mike. Joanne tells me that anything I do is okay with her. I needed another opinion before I call the gentleman back. A mutual friend told him I was thinking of buying a plane and gave him my phone number. The plane is in Florida, and I thought maybe you, Mary, Joanne, and I could go look at it this weekend."

"What about Jesse? Don't you think he'd want to go? Besides the girls may have something else in mind for the weekend."

"I want it to be a surprise for Jesse if I buy it, and I don't think Joanne has any plans." Mack starts drumming his fingers on the arm of his chair. "Even if the girls do have plans, would you go with me?"

"Sure, Mack, if Mary's plans don't include me."

"Good. Let's go ask them." Mack and Mike rise from the chairs and go back to the living room.

Entering the kitchen Mack is the first to speak, "We got tired of waiting for our second cup of coffee and decided to join you since we are the forgotten husbands."

Joanne rises and kisses him on the cheek. "You know better than that. We were so interested in the photos and Jesse talking about how he'd like to learn to take better pictures from a plane. We simply forgot that the way to a man's heart is through his stomach, and you have to keep them fed to maintain the interest." They all laugh.

Sitting down Mike asks, "Mary, what are our plans for this weekend?"

Blowing him a kiss she says, "We have nothing planned except buying groceries and cleaning the apartment, why?

"Mack and I were talking about taking you girls on a surprise trip."

Jesse speaks up, "I guess that means I'm not invited."

Mack winks at Joanne and says, "Son, we've had you under our feet since our marriage, including our honeymoon. Don't you think it's time to turn you out on your own for a couple of days? We want to see how good a job Joanne did raising you."

"That's okay, Dad. I'll see how many guys and girls I can get to come to MY unsupervised party Saturday night."

"In that case," Joanne says, "whatever your dad has planned will have to wait until you're 40 years old. Can't have you getting into trouble."

Jesse laughs and says, "I'm leaving. I know when I'm not wanted." He walks to the door turns, bows, and sweeps his arm dramatically. "Good bye, sweet people. I'll see you later."

As soon as they hear Jesse close his bedroom door, Mack says in a hushed voice, "I would like to take a fast trip to Jacksonville this weekend. I want to buy Jesse a plane for graduation, and there is a 1951 Piper Tri Pacer for sale at Herlong Airport. Mike has agreed to go with me if Mary doesn't have plans. So is it okay with you, Joanne?"

Looking thoughtful, Joanne purses her lips and says, "On one condition only. We get to go."

Mary looking startled says, "After the last flight I took I'm not so sure I ever want to look at a plane again."

Mack asks, "Mike, should we tell them that we're just looking not flying?"

"If we want them to go it might be a good idea," Mike answers. "But on the other hand, we might have a better time if we went alone."

"Neither mind," Mary says. "We're going. What time are we leaving? Will we leave Friday or Saturday?"

"Let's leave Friday about 5:00," Mack tells them.

"Okay," they all agree.

Chapter 41

Driving up to the office at Herlong Airport, Mack says, "I'll go in and see if Mr. Zimmerman is in. If he is then I'll come get you, okay?"

Mike answers, "Yes. I'm sure the girls won't mind."

Mack leaves and returns shortly. He gets into the car and says, "Mr. Zimmerman will be here in a minute, and we'll follow him to the hangar."

Joanne remarks, "I feel like a kid waiting for Santa Claus. I hope he hurries up."

"Me too," Mary says. "I've never looked at a used airplane or a new one before. I guess I should've done some research on what to look for, but I was so excited about coming I didn't. It's too late now."

Mack says, "Yes, it is, but both Mike and I did the research, and we agree that this is the right size for what I want for Jesse."

An old Army jeep pulls up beside them, and a very well dressed, tall gentleman gets out and comes over to the car. "Hello, Mr. Stevens?"

"Yes," Mack answers, "and you must be Mr. Zimmerman."

"I am, and if you will follow me, I'll show you the plane."

"Okay."

Walking into the hangar, Joanne gasps, "It's beautiful. I love the red and white paint. It looks like it is brand new. They didn't fly very much, did they?"

Mr. Zimmerman laughs and answers, "Yes, Mr. Smart flew quite a lot. He was an aerial photographer, and he took pictures not only in Florida but in Georgia and Alabama also. He was quite in demand for his photos. Sometimes he would take pictures as far away as Alaska."

Mack asks, "Then why does he want to sell? The price is so inexpensive."

Mr. Zimmerman lowers his eyes and hesitates for a minute before answering. "Mr. Smart died about six months ago. Mrs. Smart doesn't fly, and she needs the money. I shouldn't tell you that because you'll try to lower the price. I will say I won't let anyone take advantage of her."

Mack blushes and says, "I wouldn't try to lower the price unless I thought the plane would need additional work."

Straightening his shoulders and puffing out his chest, Mr. Zimmerman says, "I've been the main mechanic on this plane since Mr. Smart bought it brand new in '51. Either you want it, or you don't. I have other things to do."

Mack looks shocked. He extends his hand and says, "I'm sorry. I didn't mean to offend you. I've never looked for a plane before and was afraid maybe you were just the salesman. I didn't realize you were the mechanic. Please accept my apology."

"I guess I'm a little touchy. Mr. Smart and I grew up together, and his death was very hard on me. I'm a widower, and I never had children so I'm all alone now. At my age I'll have a tough time finding another job. All I know is flying and how to maintain a plane."

Mack looks at Joanne, and she nods her head yes. He says, "Would it be too much of an imposition to ask you to take us for a spin?"

Laughing, Mr. Zimmerman says, "I'd love to take you for a short flight. You take a car for a spin, but a plane is always a flight. This plane will seat four comfortably and five in an emergency. So come on and let's put on the parachutes and get going."

Mack and Joanne hang back from the others as they walk to the area for the parachutes. Mack says, "Hon, what do you think?"

"I like the plane, and I like Mr. Zimmerman. I think he is telling the truth, and I have a suggestion."

"Well, don't keep me hanging. What is your suggestion?"

Joanne stops, takes Mack's hand and says, "Honey, I know the vehicle will have to be financed, but I think it's a good deal for both you and Jesse." She hesitates and then continues, "Mr. Smart was an aerial photographer, and Jesse wants to try his hand at being one. Why don't we ask Mrs. Smart to include his photo equipment for an extra $100? Also, since Mr. Zimmerman will be out of a job when we buy the plane and he has no ties here, maybe he would consider becoming our mechanic."

Grabbing her and giving her a big kiss Mack says, “I know I’m the luckiest guy in the world. Your suggestions are my rule of thumb to handle life. Yes. Yes to both suggestions.”

Mr. Zimmerman is waiting patiently on them to put their parachutes on and calls, “I’m sure glad this isn’t a commercial flight because you’d still be on the ground waving goodbye to the plane.”

“Sorry, Mr. Zimmerman,” Mack says. “Joanne was giving me advice on how to act, and you know how wives get when you don’t listen.”

“Yes, I do,” Mr. Zimmerman answers.

***

“The flight was easy, and I can’t believe how quiet the engine is,” Mack says as he exits the plane.

Mike walks to Mack’s side and tells him, “I’ve never been in a plane before, but if I had the money I’d learn to fly just to buy this plane.”

“Thanks, Mike,” Mack says. “I intend to do just that.”

When Mr. Zimmerman exits the plane, Mack and Joanne walk over to him. “Mr. Zimmerman, I will buy the plane at Mrs. Smart’s price on one condition. I want her to include all of her husband’s photo equipment. Naturally I expect to pay for the equipment, say $100. Do you think she’ll accept the offer?”

Mr. Zimmerman scratches his head and says, “I know she’ll sell the plane to you. I’m not sure about the photo equipment. I can call her and let you know in a few minutes.”

“Good,” Mack says. “While you’re calling her, we’ll go have a cup of coffee. We’ll see you in about an hour.”

“Okay,” Mr. Zimmerman says, and they go their separate ways.

Meeting with Mr. Zimmerman in an hour, Mack shakes his hand and says, “What is the good word? Did she agree to sell us the plane and the photo equipment?”

Looking away from the group and twisting his hands Mr. Zimmerman says, “Yes and no. She wants to meet your son before she sells the equipment. She won’t consider another buyer until she meets him.”

“Fair enough,” Mack states. “I was going to ask if we could keep the plane here for a few weeks as it is a surprise for my son. Of course we intend to pay the storage and your maintenance fees.

Jesse could meet with Mrs. Smart at that time."

Mr. Zimmerman looks startled and says, "You want me to stay here with the plane until you pick it up?"

"Yes, and we'll need a mechanic when we take it home. Would you be willing to move and work for us?"

"Wellll, I don't know about that," Mr. Zimmerman says while running his hand through his hair. "What kind of salary are we talking about?"

"Here's what we propose: We'll pay the same amount you get now with a raise in six months. We'll pay all moving expenses and transportation to Louisville, and we'll pay your first month's rent on either an apartment or rooming house, whichever you prefer."

"I don't have to think it over," Mr. Zimmerman says. "You've got yourself a mechanic."

Chapter 42

"Dad," Jesse says as he enters the den, "I need to talk to you about something. Mom told me I had to be a man and tell you myself."

Mack looks up from his paper, and with a twinkle in his eye, says, "Don't tell me you and Diane should get married right away."

"No, Dad, that's not it. Both Diane and I want to wait until we're married before we think about anything else. I've gotten all the acceptance letters back from the universities. I didn't tell you and Mom about the junior college I applied to. I really didn't think they would accept me because they are small and have very few Bachelor of Arts degrees. Mostly they offer two-year associate degrees. However, Dad, this is where I want to go."

"Son, this is your future we're talking about, and I really think you should go to a university that will prepare you properly."

"That's the reason I didn't tell you until now. I was afraid you'd take the attitude that I should go to a school of your choice and not mine." He starts to walk out of the room.

Mack says, "Don't go. Let's talk about it some more. Tell me the name of the college and why you want to attend. Then we'll make a decision. Come on, Jesse, act like a man. Sit down, and let's talk."

Coming back into the room Jesse sits down and says, "You know I think I want to be a commercial pilot. I also want to explore aerial photography. Jacksonville Junior College has a two-year associate degree for most careers. They have a business degree, and that is what I'm most interested in. Eventually I want to start my own charter airplane business, and if I decide to do the aerial photography I will need to know how to run both businesses. Of course there is an ulterior motive. The college is close to the Herlong Airport. Herlong was built during WWII to train the Navy and Air Force pilots. After the war the airport was given to the Jacksonville Aviation Authority, and it is the leading pilot training school in the nation. See, Dad, I'd be getting the training for the commercial pilot's license, learning how to take aerial photos, and working toward a degree in business."

"Jesse," Mack says, "I'm so very proud of you, and like your mother I want to think about it for a while before I give an answer. Why don't you tell Joanne that we'll discuss this after supper?"

"Okay, Dad, I will." Jesse rises and leaves the room.

***

Setting down his coffee cup and looking at Jesse, Mack says, "I promised we'd talk about your choice of schools tonight. First let me say that I have discussed the issue with Joanne, and we both agree we want what is best for you. I'd like to know how you found out about Jacksonville Junior College and also who told you the history of Herlong Airport."

Jesse shrugs his shoulders and answers, "It hasn't been a secret that I want to be a commercial pilot and a couple of guys in my class are thinking of joining the Air Force in the hopes of being selected to learn to fly. I could go to one of the Ivy League colleges, join the R.O.T.C., and pray the Air Force would teach me to take aerial photos. However, that is a big chance I'd be taking, and I don't want to risk it. Mr. O'Brien told me about Herlong, and I checked into colleges close to the air field. I like the fact that Jacksonville Junior College is close, and most of the students of the Herlong Flight School are students at the college. Don't you see, I'd be with other students who have the same interests as me. I would learn so much more there than anywhere else. Please, Dad, let me go there."

Joanne asks, "Since the airport is a teaching school would you need your own plane, or do they furnish one for you?"

"I'm sorry, Mom, but I forgot to ask that. If you'll excuse me I'll make a phone call and get the answer."

"Sure, Son," Mack says, "make the call. I'd like that answer also."

Jumping up from the chair Jesse rushes over and kisses Joanne on the cheek then he runs from the room and up the stairs.

Laughing, Mack states, "He didn't think of using the phone in the kitchen."

"No," Joanne says, "he was too excited to think of anything except getting the information to convince us to let him go to

Florida."

Jesse comes back into the room, and before anyone can speak he says, "I can either have my own plane or pay a fee to use one of the rentals that is kept at the airfield. Do you have any other questions? Would you like to talk to each other without me? If you would I'll go to my room until you call me down."

"Son, I'm convinced that you have made a wise and informed choice. My vote is to let you go to Jacksonville Junior College and continue your flight instruction at Herlong."

Joanne says, "I agree with your father."

Jesse jumps up, runs to his father and throws his arms around him; then he runs to Joanne, kisses her on the cheek, and says, "I love you both! Thanks for letting me go to Jacksonville Junior College!"

Looking very stern, Mack shakes a finger at Jesse and says, "Joanne and I have a surprise for you, and you just ruined it. Never mind, Son, we still love you. Take a seat, and we'll tell you all about it."

Jesse sits down, and Mack tells him, "We bought a plane, and right now it's at Herlong. We had planned to bring it home the weekend after your graduation. The big question is do you want to keep it there, or shall we bring it home for my use?"

Jesse looks puzzled and asks, "Why did you buy a plane? Did you intend to fly to see me every weekend because you were going to miss me or to spy on me?"

Joanne speaks up, "We bought it so you could use it when you want to take the pictures, and, yes, we did want to visit you on campus. Since you will be going to a flight school you have to decide if you want the plane with you and fly home when you can or if you want to rent a plane, and we can fly down to see you."

With a twinkle in his eye and a very serious look, Jesse answers, "I don't see why you couldn't buy two planes. Then I wouldn't have to make a decision."

Mack and Joanne look at each other and start laughing. Mack says, "My son, we wanted you to start facing the problems of the world. Think about what you want to do and let us know. We have about a week before graduation. Okay?"

"Sure, Dad," Jesse says as he gets up and starts for the door. Turning he asks, "It's okay for me to leave isn't it?"

Nodding, they say, "Yes."

"What do you think, Joanne? Should we leave the plane there

for Jesse, or should we bring it here and let him rent a plane?"

Joanne things for a moment and then answers, "I think we should check the prices first, and then we can make a wise decision."

"You're right. Will you do that tomorrow?"

"Yes, Love, I will." She rises, kisses Mack and leaves the room.

Chapter 43

"I can't wait for Dad to get home," Jesse says as he reaches for a cookie. "I know he will understand my decision about the plane once I tell him what I found out during my phone call."Joanne is sitting at the table and says, "I'm glad you have made a decision. I'm sure that we all will have something exciting to tell after supper."

"Mom, I'm so excited that I don't think I could study if I tried. Would it be okay if I went over to Diane's until supper? That is, if her mother doesn't mind.

"Go ahead, Jesse, and call her. I don't need you underfoot, pacing the floor and disturbing me all afternoon."

"Thanks, Mom," Jesse calls over his shoulder as he heads for the stairs.

***

"The supper was good as usual," Mack says as he rises from the table and looks at Jesse. "Come on, Jesse, let's go to the den while Joanne cleans the kitchen."

"Sorry, Love," Joanne says, "I'm going to let the kitchen go for a few minutes while we all talk about our day. Okay?"

"Sure," Mack says and he starts for the den with Jesse and Joanne close on his heels.

After they all sit down, Mack says, "Okay who wants to go first? I can't tell who is the most excited or who is champing at the bit to tell their news first."

Joanne looks at Jesse and says, "Jesse went over to Diane's this afternoon because he was too excited to study. How about it, Son, will you go first?"

"Yes, Mom, I will. I checked with the flight school, and the instructor I spoke to said that very few of the students have their own plane. He suggested that I not keep my plane, as the fees for the instructor and the plane are included in the tuition. Besides, I'd be at a disadvantage when meeting the other guys with my plane there. They would think I was trying to be better than they are."

Mack says, "That you would, Son. So we'll bring the plane here, and then we can spy on you by just showing up some weekend."

"That's fine, Dad, if you bring Diane with you. Like you and Mom, she was a little disappointed that I didn't go to the same school she chose. I feel good about my choice, and I think it won't be long after graduation that I'll have my own business with several employees."

"Oh, Jesse," Joanne exclaims, eyes glowing, "I'm so glad you have a dream, and we'll do everything we can to help you realize it!

"Now for my news. It isn't quite as exciting, but I have the figures for the storage space and a room for Mr. Zimmerman. I also called the Aviation Board and requested the forms to fill out for both the license for the plane and for you, Mack. I figure the school will certify Jesse, so I didn't ask for him. The forms should be here within the next couple of days.

"I called Mrs. Smart, and she is willing to rent a room to Jesse ... if he wants it. Her house is close to the airport, and she said she'd love to have him stay. Besides she still has the photo equipment, and we wouldn't have to move it twice."

"Mom, you're the greatest. I never thought about where I'd stay. I think that's a great idea. What about the photo equipment?"

Mack says, "Another surprise. We found out that Mrs. Smart's husband was an aerial photographer and negotiated with her for his equipment. We were going to pick it up when we picked up the plane. It does make sense to leave it with Mrs. Smart since you will be staying there, doesn't it?"

"Sure does," Jesse answers. "I can't wait to get started. I want to tell Diane. I know she'll be happy for me."

"Go ahead and call her," Mack says. "I think we've told you everything now." He picks up his paper to read, and Jesse leaves the room.

Chapter 44

Mrs. Smart meets them at the door and says, "You must be the Stevens, and you have to be Jesse."

"Yes, we are," Mack answers. "Sorry to be so late but we didn't get started as soon as we hoped."

"Come in. That's okay. I started either a late dinner or an early supper. It'll be ready in about a half an hour. In the meantime I'll show you to your rooms, and you can relax for awhile before we eat."

"Good," Joanne says. "Jesse can unpack, and when supper is over he'll be ready to ask questions."

"It's good to have a young man in the house again." Mrs. Smart says as she wipes a tear from her eye. "My son was a pilot in the Air Force, and he was shot down over Korea. They still don't know if he was killed or if he was taken prisoner. I pray for his safety and hope he was taken prisoner."

Joanne remarks, "I'm so sorry. I'm glad that Jesse can fill the loneliness for you."

Mack takes Joanne by the hand and says, "Please show us to our rooms, and we'll finish this conversation after awhile."

"Yes, of course," Mrs. Smart says as she starts for the stairs. "Please follow me."

***

Jesse is the first to come into the kitchen. "Something smells good."

"Thank you, Jesse," Mrs. Smart replies. "I hope you all like it. It's called goulash, and it's a specialty of mine. My husband required it once a week. He said it made him wise and strong."

Jesse says, "I'll keep that in mind and when I start feeling sluggish, I'll request you make it."

She laughs and says, "I'll look forward to you telling me which of my meals you like the best."

Mack and Joanne join them, and Joanne asks, "May I help you with anything?"

"Sure," Mrs. Smart answers, "you may set the table. The dishes are in the cabinet, and since I'm serving goulash, we'll need soup bowls, large spoons, and forks for dessert. The spoons are in the drawer under the dishes. Napkins are on the counter."

Joanne salutes her, walks to the cabinet and says, "Aye, aye, sir."

Mack laughs and asks, "What can I do?"

Laughing with him, Mrs. Smart answers, "The newspaper is on the couch. Why don't you go sit down and read for about 10 minutes."

"That sounds like a winner to me." Mack says as he leaves the room.

***

"Come and get it." Joanne calls.

In a small voice and high pitched, Mack answers, "Coming, Mother."

They all laugh, and Jesse winks at Mrs. Smart and says, "Now you see why I'm so anxious to leave these two. They'd drive anyone to the far corners of the earth."

"They'll be leaving soon, and then we'll see what mischief you can get into. I feel like I'm part of the family."

Joanne reaches for her hand, reaches for Mack's hand and says, "Let's say grace and then eat."

Jesse takes Mack's hand and Mrs. Smart's hand.

Everyone bows their heads, and Mack says, "Thank You, Lord, for the food set before us. Let it nourish our bodies and our souls. Keep Jesse safe in his new environment, and let us have a safe trip home. Bless Mrs. Smart and her generous heart. Amen."

They say in unison, "Amen."

As they are doing dishes, Joanne says, "I'm sure Mack would like the goulash sometimes. Would you give me the recipe?

"Be glad to," Mrs. Smart replies, laughing. "But if I didn't give it to you then you'd have to come back more often."

"You and Jesse will probably see us more than you want to

anyway. Mack will want to see how Jesse is coming along with his lessons."

Mrs. Smart reaches over and touches Joanne's hand and says, "Well, believe me when I say you are welcome anytime for as long as you want to stay."

"Thank you."

Mrs. Smart says, "Let's go to the living room for coffee. I've arranged a small surprise for Jesse, and I want you and Mack to see it also."

Mack raises his hand and states, "We don't expect you to go out of your way to accommodate Jesse. He's a big boy and needs to be on his own."

She starts to protest, "I know, but ..." The doorbell interrupts her thought. She opens the door and says, "Come in, Doc."

Mack rises, shakes Doc Zimmerman's hand, and says, "This is a surprise. I thought we'd take Jesse out to see the plane tomorrow morning and introduce him to you then. By the way, Jesse, this is Mr. Zimmerman."

Jesse rises and shakes his hand. "It's good to meet you, Mr. Zimmerman. I can't wait to start school and learn how to take aerial photos."

"Would anyone like a cup of coffee?" Mrs. Smart asks.

Doc looks at her and winks, "I'll take a cup after awhile but not now."

Taking their cue from Doc both Mack and Joanne say, "No."

Doc and Mrs. Smart start to sit down when the doorbell rings. Mrs. Smart says, "Sit down, Doc and I'll see who is at the door."

Opening the door, she sees a gentleman in uniform. "Hello, may I help you?" she asks.

"Yes, ma'am. I'm supposed to meet Doc Zimmerman here."

"Doc is here," she answers. "Won't you come in?"

Rising, Doc walks over and shakes his hand. Turning to the others he says, "I want you to meet Captain Darrell Rush. Captain Rush will be teaching Jesse the method of taking photos from a plane. Darrell, this is Jesse; his parents Mack and Joanne Stevens; and Mrs. Smart opened the door for you."

Jesse rushes forward and shakes his hand. Gushing, he says, "I'm so glad to meet you. I can't wait to start my lessons."

Captain Rush says, "Good. It's great to meet your parents and to see your enthusiasm. I'll be talking to you next week after you've gotten settled and know what your schedule will be."

Joanne looks at Doc and says, "I don't know how we could ever thank you and Mrs. Smart for all the help you've given Jesse."

Mrs. Smart nods and says, "It's the least we can do for the privilege of getting to know a fine, upstanding young man like your son."

"Enough of this chatter," Doc states. "Grace, I'm ready for that cup of coffee. That is, if the offer still stands."

Laughing Mrs. Smart rises and says, "Come join me in the kitchen, Joanne. I think we are being dismissed."

Chapter 45

Lying on the beach, Joanne turns to Mack and says, "I'm so glad you bought the plane. I wasn't sure at first but it's fun flying with you and seeing the different towns even when I have to explore alone. This is the best. I've enjoyed Hawaii so much."

"Yes, Honey, it has been fun. I've been planning our second honeymoon since our first. Did you know this is the first trip we've taken without Jesse? When I told him I was taking you to Hawaii, he looked at me and said, 'Without me?' I told him this was our honeymoon as he horned in on our first one."

Laughing, Joanne asks, "What did he say to that?"

"Plenty after he quit sputtering. He told me to take lots of pictures and not to throw you down a volcano. I told him I'd never do that especially since I've gotten used to your cooking."

Joanne props her head on her hand, looks him in the eye and says very seriously, "So now I'm just a cook and bottle washer."

Grabbing her Mack says, "Don't even think that. I don't think I could survive if anything happened to you. I know Jesse would have a hard time."

She kisses Mack and tells him, "We better go in and get ready. Remember we're going to a luau this afternoon."

"Are you going to learn the hula?"

"Maybe," she says with a twinkle in her eye. "I was thinking about some private lessons so I could entertain our guests when we get back home."

"If you do learn it, what makes you think I'd let you perform for our guests?"

Laughing she states, "I thought you might want them to see what I learned."

"Nope. That entertainment would be for me exclusively."

"Okay, you made your point," Joanne says as she starts to walk away.

Mack calls, “Hey, wait for me!”

Joanne turns, laughs, and says, “Catch me if you can,” and starts running away.

***

Joanne is pouring Jesse a cup of coffee and tells him, “It’s good to have you home.”

He answers, “It’s good to be home. I’m going over to see Diane in a few minutes, but I’ll be back in time for supper. Okay?”

“Of course it’s okay. Why don’t you ask her to come to supper? We haven’t seen her since you’ve been in school.”

“I will, Mom.” Jesse plays with his cup, raises his head and says, “I’m planning to ask her to marry me after I graduate. Do you think she will? I’d hate to be disappointed. What if she says no? What would I do then?

Walking over to him, she puts her hand on his shoulder and says, “If God intends for you and Diane to marry, she’ll say yes, but if it isn’t meant to be she’ll say maybe or no. Keep your faith in God and always trust His judgment. When do you expect to ask her?”

“I thought I’d take her to some place special and ask her over supper. Do you have any suggestions?”

“Well, your dad took me to Kunz’s and then we took a walk. I remember his holding my hand, and we didn’t say a word for several blocks. Then he told me that he hadn’t thought he could ever feel about any woman the way he felt about your mother. He said I was very close to the same feeling, and if I thought I could stand him and you he’d like for me to consider marrying him. Not very romantic, but I told him I’d think about it. The rest is history.”

“You know what, Mom? I think I’ll take her to Fountain Ferry Park and propose in the Old Mill. It’s dark, and we’d be on the boat ride. She wouldn’t be able to see how nervous I’ll be, and I wouldn’t be able to see the expression on her face. That’s what I’ll do.” Rising from the chair and walking towards the door he turns, walks to Joanne, kisses her on the cheek, and says, “Thanks, Mom and please don’t say anything to her or Dad about this.”

She laughs, “I wouldn’t dare. Just be sure to bring her with you when you announce it to us.”

“I will.”

Chapter 46

Looking up from his paper, Mack asks, “Where did Jesse and Diane go tonight?”

“They went to Fontaine Ferry. I don’t expect Jesse home until much later.”

“We haven’t seen very much of him, and when we do he has Diane with him. Do you suppose it’s serious?”

Joanne puts her book down, blows him a kiss, and says, “I, for one, wouldn’t object if it was. I hope she feels the same way about him.”

“Joanne, I think he’s too young to even think about getting serious. I’m not ready to be an in-law yet. Do you think I could talk him into seeing other girls?”

“No, I don’t think you could. Anyway, Diane has been around for quite a few years, and I’m used to her. You want to keep Jesse a little boy.” She goes over and sits on Mack’s lap. “Would you have listened when you asked his mother to marry you?”

He kisses her and answers, “No, but I was a few years older and was already starting up the ladder of success at the bank.”

“How do you know Jesse isn’t ready and starting up his own ladder of success?”

“I don’t. Guess I’ll have to trust God to help him make the right decision. Won’t I?”

“Yes, you will.”

The door opens, and Jesse and Diane walk into the room. They both look like the cat who ate the canary. Jesse is the first to speak, “Dad, Mom, I want you to meet the future Mrs. Jesse Stevens.”

Joanne jumps up and rushes to Diane. “Welcome! I’m so happy we’ll have you in our family.” She gives her a big hug, and, turning to Jesse, she hugs him. Before she can say anything to Jesse, Mack shakes his hand and hugs Diane.

"I'm glad to see Jesse has the sense to propose to a very beautiful and smart girl. I'm looking forward to being an in-law. When is the wedding taking place?"

Jesse and Diane sit down on the couch, and Jesse says, "We're not sure of a date, but the wedding will be after I graduate. That will be in another year and a half. I'll be counting the days."

Diane blushes and says, "We have to tell my parents in a little while, but we wanted to tell you first. I'd like for you, Mrs. Stevens, to help me with the guest list, and please feel free to give me any suggestions."

"Diane, I'm sure your mother will want to help you, and she may resent me giving you suggestions. Let's play it by ear. I'll do anything you and your mother want me to do to help."

"Thanks, Mrs. Stevens. We'll talk about this a little later, but now I think we'd better see my parents. Don't you, Jesse?"

"Yes, I do. I'll see you all later." The kids walk out the door.

Mack looks at Joanne very sternly and asks, "You knew he was going to ask her to marry him, didn't you?"

"Yes, but Jesse didn't want you to know until after he asked her because if she said no he didn't want you to know he'd been rejected."

"Come here, vixen."

She does, and he gives her a big kiss and hug.

Chapter 47

Joanne pours Diane a cup of coffee and says, "I'm so glad you came over today. I was feeling a little blue with both Mack and Jesse gone."

"I've been planning to come to see you because I needed to get away from all the wedding talk. Mother has taken over, and there isn't much I can do except nod my head and say, 'Yes, I like it very much,' or 'Yes, I think that will work.' I really wanted to talk about the honeymoon." Laughing, she adds, "No, you and Mack are not invited. No arguments! Just because you took Jesse on your honeymoon isn't a good enough reason for us to take you on ours."

Looking very serious Joanne states, "I've picked out the outfits to wear on your honeymoon, and now you tell me I can't go. I'm so disappointed." They both laugh.

Joanne says, "The best trip we took was to Hawaii. We stayed right on the ocean, and Mack took me on moonlit walks on the beach. The hotel had a swimming pool, and we could walk into the ocean. The ocean is so clear we could see the bottom. From a distance you could see where the deep part began and the shallow part stopped. There were two different shades of blue. The sun shone the whole time we were there, and there was a gentle breeze blowing. It never got to the point where you were uncomfortable walking or doing any other exercise.

"The hotel had karaoke every night or dancing. The people were very friendly. Lots of shopping, and the beauty can't be described. There are lots of things to do and see. We didn't have a dull moment, and we'd been married for five years.

"The other trip I'd put at the top of my list was the cruise to the Bahamas. We didn't stay in Freeport. We went to Belle Channel. The hotel wasn't in our usual category, but it and the people were nice. When I saw it I thought it was about to fall down, or they were tearing it down. It had all the windows and doors open.

Again, we walked, but were warned not to walk at night. The native shows were great, and we explored the native cuisine. We took a guided tour and saw a man-made botanical garden.

"We took a cruise to the eastern Caribbean, which was fun, educational and relaxing. It was for 14 days, and we could eat any kind of food we wanted 24 hours a day. They had a theme for every night and a floor show. The shows were good, and ..." The phone rings, and Joanne says, "Excuse me, it might be Mack."

Diane is watching Joanne's facial expressions as she answers the phone.

"Hello.

"Yes, this is she.

"He left day before yesterday to attend a meeting with the officers of Chase Bank in New York. He isn't due home until late this afternoon.

"That sounds like his plane."

Bursting into tears she sits down, and with her free hand she covers her mouth.

Dianne rushes to her with a handkerchief and stands by her side.

"Yes, yes, I'll be right down. Thank you for calling." Joanne hangs up the phone and bursts into full fledged crying.

Diane doesn't know what to say or do, so she just stands beside her, puts her arm around her, and holds her tight.

Joanne finally quits crying and says, "I'm sorry. That was the state police. Mack was on his way home when he ran into a storm. A lightning bolt hit the engine, and he crashed." Breaking into tears again she stammers, "He's dead. I can't believe he's dead. They want me to come down and identify both the plane and him. Diane, will you go with me?"

"Of course I will, and while you change your clothes I'll call Jesse and have mother bring me some clothes. I'm staying here with you until Jesse gets home."

***

Mack is flying home when he hits a rain storm. He thinks, *I'll soon be out of this. They didn't mention severe weather so it's just a gentle rain. I sure wish my arm would quit hurting. When I get home I'm going to mention it to Joanne and see a doctor. Oh! The lightning has hit the engine and it's on fire! I'll have to jump.* He reaches for the radio and says, “Mayday! Mayday! My plane has been hit by lightning. I’m jumping shortly. I’ll try not to hit any buildings with the plane. Over and out.”

***

“Mrs. Stevens, we are releasing your husband’s body to the funeral home. The autopsy showed your husband suffered a major heart attack. It must have happened when the plane caught fire. I’m so very sorry. If there is anything we can do please feel free to call us.”

Chapter 48

Looking out over the creek, the three are silent. Suddenly Tom says, "I can't believe after all these years the tree and the creek haven't changed one iota. Can you?"

Joanne looks at Mary and says, "It seems strange being here without Mack. He always wanted to see where I grew up, and I always had an excuse not to bring him. I think I was ashamed to let him see how poor I was."

Mary puts her hand on Joanne's arm and tells her, "We have come a long way since we made the vow to become millionaires, haven't we?"

Tom and Joanne say, "Yes, we have."

Shaking her head, Joanne hands a check to each of them and says, "Here is your share of the insurance money. Tom, I never want to see or hear from you again."

"Joanne, you don't mean that." Tom exclaims with shock in his voice. "I had nothing to do with Mack's death, and you know that."

"Only by the Grace of God, Mack insisted on going to New York by private plane. I tried to talk him out of it, but no, he had to be there within two hours. The plane crashed somewhere in the Smokys. It has been a nightmare for both Jesse and me. Neither of us can sleep or eat. I thought maybe this would be a place for both of us to renew our faith in God and find peace."

Mary nods her head and, taking Joanne in her arms, says, "You will, and because Jesse has you, he will also."

"What about our plans to marry a year after Mack's death?" Tom asks.

"They were your plans, Tom, not mine. I do not intend to ever marry again. Mack was the love of my life. Sure, I'll be lonely at times, but I can assure you it won't be for you! After we get back to Louisville, I don't want to ever see you or hear from you again."

"Joanne," Tom says as he hangs his head, "I've never found

another model who could pose as well as you. You're so photogenic, and you've always been in demand. Won't you change your mind and at least model for me?"

"No, Tom. Jesse is my priority, and all my time will be devoted to him and the various organizations I'm involved with. There isn't room for modeling, or you, or anyone else."

With that statement, Mary speaks up, "Does that include me?"

"Mary, no. I want you and Mike to be a part of Jesse's and my life. He will need a man's guiding hand, and I think Mike is just the person to do that."

"Thanks for the compliment. Mike will be pleased to know he can do things with Jesse."

Getting up and walking away, Tom says, "We will run into each other at different functions, and I will change your mind, Joanne."

"I don't think so," Joanne states. "Jesse and I don't need your kind around us. I haven't heard about you since you cut the ripcord on Mack's parachute. I thought perhaps you had realized that Mack was the only man for me and you moved away."

Tom looks at Joanne and says, "The investigation caused everyone to doubt me. I couldn't get another girl to pose for me, and the companies started asking for anyone but me to take their photos. Finally I didn't have anywhere to turn except to come back to the mountains. After I arrived, I started taking photos of the animals and scenery and writing small inserts to go with the pictures. I submitted them to nature, camping, and children's magazines. I've become quite well known for both the photos and the stories. In fact *National Geographic* has asked me to do the pictures for one of its feature stories. I will be paid the same salary as I was for the photos I took of you. I will also be given an expense account and a bonus. Things are looking up for my future ... with or without you.

"I've dreamt of Mack's death and you marrying me. Now you tell me that can never be. I have the money you promised when we were kids, but it doesn't mean a thing without you. God, I wish I could turn back the clock."

Joanne looks at Tom, gives her hair a twist, and says, "Tom, at one time I loved you like a brother. Things changed, and I fell in love with Mack. You couldn't or wouldn't accept this and tried to destroy my happiness for your own selfish reasons. Your acts against Mack destroyed any and all feelings I had for you. When we're finished here I never want to see or hear from you again. Do you understand?"

Standing, Mary says, "I feel the same way Tom. You're not the man I knew as a boy. Anyway, I have a bit of news, and to say Mike is excited is putting it mildly."

Tom and Joanne both look at Mary and Joanne asks, "What is the news? Are you buying a house? What?"

Blushing and looking at the ground Mary answers, "Mike and I decided to give Joanne another project to keep her busy. We're going to have a baby."

Rushing to Mary, Joanne puts her arms around her and gushes, "That's the best news I've heard today. As soon as we get back, let's start planning the nursery. I guess you'll be looking for a house also?"

"We put a bid on one two days ago. We should know something when we get back."

"That's great," Joanne says, "Jesse will be thrilled, and I know he'll want to take all the baby pictures. He and Diane have set their wedding date, and you will get an invitation."

Tom starts to leave, turns, and says, "I can't stay and listen to you two talk about your futures when I don't have one. Someday, Joanne, when you get fed up with living alone, give me a call. I might still be interested in you, but don't hold your breath. I'm going to marry the first girl that'll have me."

"That's a good intention, Tom." Joanne answers, "You should have done that a long time ago."

About the Author

Teddi has lived in Southern Indiana all her life. She started writing professionally after taking a couple of Creative Writing Courses at Indiana University Southeast. She has also attended several writing conferences.

Her father was a minister and Teddi took his sermons to heart. She hopes her books are an inspiration to everyone. She tells everybody, "I hope my books brings back a lot of happy memories for anyone living during World War II; and may the books help the young people cope with their loved ones leaving for combat duty."

CPSIA information can be obtained at www.ICGtesting.com
Printed in the USA
LVOW120803161112

307592LV00001B/22/P